D0519165

90710 000 473 431

WE WERE
WOLVES

WE WERE WOLVES

Written and illustrated by
JASON COCKCROFT

ANDERSEN PRESS

First published in 2021 by
Andersen Press Limited
20 Vauxhall Bridge Road
London SW1V 2SA
www.andersenpress.co.uk

2 4 6 8 10 9 7 5 3 1

All rights reserved. No part of this publication may be reproduced,
stored in a retrieval system or transmitted in any form, or by any means,
electronic, mechanical, photocopying, recording or otherwise,
without the written permission of the publisher.

The right of Jason Cockcroft to be identified as the author and illustrator
of this work has been asserted by him in accordance with
the Copyright, Designs and Patents Act, 1988.

Copyright © Jason Cockcroft, 2021

Epigraph from *East of Eden* by John Steinbeck, published by Penguin Classics.
East of Eden copyright © John Steinbeck, 1952
Published by Viking Press 1952, William Heinemann Ltd 1952, Penguin Books 1992,
2000, 2017.
Reproduced with kind permission of Penguin Books Ltd.

British Library Cataloguing in Publication Data available.

ISBN 978 1 83913 057 1

Printed and bound in Italy by Elcograf S.p.A.

This book is dedicated to
Alan Cockcroft,
my father.

LONDON BOROUGH OF RICHMOND UPON THAMES	
90710 000 473 431	
Askews & Holts	14-May-2021
JF TEENAGE 11-14	
RTTE	

There is no other story.
A man, after he has brushed off the dust
and chips of life, will have left only the hard,
clean questions: was it good or was it evil?

East of Eden, John Steinbeck

So what do you want to know?

I suppose you're expecting to hear about how I killed my dad and got away with it, and how when they found me I was nearly half dead myself, on account that he'd tried to do away with me. Except that's not what happened, of course. Not that anyone cares now. Because lies have faster legs than the truth, like Mam says. So all I can do is tell it like it happened and as I saw it, because it's our story, me and John. And now he's gone for good, so who else will tell the tale if not me?

PART ONE

ONE

IT BEGAN WITH the dog.

John always said that it was a bad idea to get too close to anything that needed you, and I suppose when the dog arrived I had a choice, and I chose wrong, that's all. I should have listened to John, but he was in prison by then, and I was alone and needed something that was just mine for once.

John was my dad's name. He never liked me calling him Dad and didn't call me son, not even when I was young and he was away in the desert making sure we were all safe, and we'd only get to talk on the phone once or twice a month. Him and Mam weren't together then, but they hadn't told anyone and certainly not me. People didn't know until he came home and started living in the woods instead of in our house. Which is when Mam started to worry. At first, he just had a sleeping bag and the few tools he needed, and it could have been a hobby, a bit of fun. But later there was the caravan, and later still, I moved in with him, and it wasn't fun any more.

I liked the caravan. In winter it smelled of mould and peat and oil from the heater, and in summer it smelled of sunlight and hot glass and wild garlic. We were next to the stream and after March the garlic choked the banks with white flowers so that the air was thick with it, sweet and heavy like nothing I'd smelled before. I didn't know anything about garlic or burdock before I lived with him, couldn't point to a nettle, even. What I knew was streetlights and pavements and locked doors and no plants and no trees. There wasn't any green on the estate. But in the woods, you learned quick, for no better reason than you had to. Sometimes it felt like a different world, away from the real things that happened, which is what John wanted, I think.

The caravan was small. It didn't have carpet or furniture, but it had a narrow room with a bed in it and a fold-out cot in the front part, a stand-up kitchen but no electricity, a toilet but no plumbing. We did our business in the woods, and took water from the stream.

It would take me five long strides to reach the stream from the door of the caravan, and three for John. But once I swear I saw him with my own eyes jump clean out of the bedroom window, straight in, just to show off. Like a man leaping for his life from a fire, but smiling as he went, which is how I like to remember him.

I'd only ever known our house, of course, and the caravan wasn't like the house, and it wasn't clean. And when it was cold it was like sleeping in a sardine can that had been kept in a fridge overnight. One week it snowed so much the roof buckled with the weight, but I liked the noise the raindrops made on the tin-sheet repair after. We were never told whose caravan it was, but we weren't the first because John found lots of papers and things stuffed in bags under the kitchen sink that he said were written in Polish, and Polish was one of the languages he knew a bit of.

'Itinerant workers,' he'd say, nodding. 'Pickers and diggers for Mr Derby. Good soldiers, too, the Poles,' he told me. 'Almost as good as Gurkhas.'

Like I say, I had no problems with the caravan, but people who weren't there tell me now that that's when it all started going wrong, with the caravan and the landowner called Mr Derby. And they say maybe if he'd only left us alone then things might not have ended like they did. But they don't know that all the things that happened and all the things that will ever happen were put in place long before the council letters were pinned to the caravan door and the men in suits came to the woods.

What happened was set out before I was born even, and before John and my mam met, and before the war, too. Before the beasts that had laid quiet under that wood for thousands of years finally climbed up out of the soil. It was all set like a sleeping stone in the earth beneath our feet long before any of us were here, like the bones of bears and wolves and wild bulls that are there if you dig deep enough.

'Things happen despite us, not because of us,' is what John would say, 'and it's pointless fighting it. There are better fights to be had,' he'd tell me, squeezing my hand and looking at me, real warm, like he thought just seeing his smile would let me know what he meant. Which it didn't, not always.

He'd been arrested for burglary, but pleaded trespass, which meant he was banged up anyway, on account of his record. That was the story, but John always said, 'If the coppers want to, they could have you locked up for as long as they want, and that's why you have to make sure you always have someone on your side with clout.' Clout meaning power, meaning money, meaning back-up.

John knew villains, see. Men with flash cars who'd come and park up on the other side of the stream, and them and John would do business while I walked through the trees and tried not to listen too hard in case I heard something I didn't like.

Some of them he got on with and some he didn't, but he always told me, 'Never turn down a chat with a bloke about a job, because you don't know if it'll bring you Gold and Stars.' Gold and Stars were always big with him, cluttering his head, like they were real rather than just ideas – because of the things he'd heard out in that desert, I suppose, and the things he'd seen. Men turned to red dust in a gunflash, and flames that spewed up from the black sand, straight like fountains. Up to the sky, black and orange and burning.

But I knew the difference.

When they took him down in the court in Leeds, he shouted over to me that he'd be gone no more than a month. So I nodded, and I walked to the bus station with the rucksack the lawyer man had given me on the street, and I got the bus back to our place in the woods, and I never thought to doubt what he said, because John was always right when it came to the coppers and the courts. And it wasn't the first time he'd been banged up, anyway, was it? On account of the other time, back before the caravan and the woods, back when I still thought we'd be a family. Me, him and Mam. So I wasn't too worried, see. I never looked in the rucksack, either, because I knew I'd find the gun there. And I didn't want anything to do with that, because guns meant Pain and Blood and Death, and as far as I was concerned John had seen enough of that already for both of us. But there are some things you can't avoid, no matter how hard you try, and I suppose men of guns always end in a bad way, and that's how it was for him, only I didn't know that then.

TWO

Sometimes, in summer, there'd be other people in the fields close by. Families playing games by their tents, cooking at night and music coming through the trees. That's where I met Sophie, but I'll talk about her later, because she didn't know anything about the dog coming, not until after it all started going bad. And I loved her, and maybe she loved me, but that's all I'll say for now.

I'd been living with John for half a year, so I already knew how to cook over the camping stove, and how not to waste the paraffin, and how to cover our tracks and stop too much smoke from rising, and find fresh food when I needed it. I could tell sorrel from lords and ladies, and hemlock from cow parsley, and I could name off the top of my head seven different mushrooms for eating.

When John was sent down it was early March, and a real nice one – mists in the first hours but the kind that burned off quick as soon as the sun came out. Most mornings back then I'd drink tea by the small pile of stones I'd press round the fire, for the heat they'd give off, and I'd wonder what we'd do when he came out of Armley Gaol and if things would be different.

Gaol meaning prison, meaning clink, meaning lock-up.

I wondered whether we'd stay in the caravan or if he had new plans – plans that would make me worried and excited at the same time. And I thought other thoughts, like how we all came to be, and how it is that men and women meet and decide to bring a kid into the world, and the magic in all that, and the recklessness, too. I thought about what it meant that some things live only as long as a day, mayflies and the like, and others survive a hundred years or more. And I thought about how when you're on your own, time sort of slows, but not in a bad way, and it gives you space to hear things clearly, birds and that.

Birds were on my mind. Before getting the bus back from Leeds, I'd gone to the big library and got a book out about birdsong and their eggs and nests, and what to look for, and by the time he came back I wanted to be able to show him I recognised nuthatch and different kinds of woodpecker. So I sat and drank the hot tea as the dew glistened on my boots and the glossy blue air filled with cobwebs, and I thought about waking next to him, and his smell, and the great bellows he made going outside to set the fire for breakfast, to clear out his chest, yelling like a muntjac deer.

While I was thinking about all this on that first afternoon alone, the dog appeared, all yellow and still, like the ground itself had spat her out, like she'd been under the earth in the roots and dirt and stones, asleep all this time and content, and only waiting for the right time to show herself to me.

Which I think, looking back, was the truth.

She was a yellow dog with short fur and a black nose and eyes that had a silvery shine when you looked close. They stared back at you and past you at the same time, which I didn't mind at all.

'Here, girl.'

She looked at me and past me, and turned.

'Come on, don't be shy.'

There was a long, narrow clearing by the caravan where we'd strip the nettles right down, John and me. Low enough so the new growth was clean and tender, instead of woody. New leaves made the best nettle tea, John said. Anyway, the dog wandered down the outside of the nettle paddock, nosed me, curious and sort of sleepy-eyed, as though having woken from a long dream. Then, seeing that I was no threat, she went back up the trail on the opposite side, through the died-back sorrel and chervil, before doing it all over again. Each time she made her round and lifted her head to look at me, it was as though she was seeing me for the first time. Gentle and helpless, and trusting.

After an hour, the dog lay down near the fire and I went over to see if she had a collar.

A small brassy disc had the name 'Molly' engraved on it.

I went to the van and got a coil of blue baling twine and tied it around the dog's neck, and tried training her to sit. But she hated the twine and shook her head so hard, trying to get it loose, that I was worried she'd hurt herself. So I gave up on tying her, and after that I never did use the twine again. Anyway, she already knew how to sit.

THREE

'JOHN SAYS YOU'RE not to open the bag, and don't tell anyone about it. Do you understand? He'll collect it when he's back. He wants to know if you're looking after yourself.'

This was the lawyer man on the phone the next day. He told me to call him Alan, but I never did call him anything. I didn't know him and didn't really want to. There were a lot of fellas I didn't want to know, more every day, I thought. I wondered where they all came from and why, because the world certainly didn't seem to have a lack of them these days.

'When's he coming back, did he say?'

'You're to stay at the caravan, and try not to show yourself too often. If you need anything, you're to call me.'

'Course,' I said. Because, I thought, where else would I go?

He must have heard the thought through the telephone wire somehow, because he said: 'There's the matter of your mother. Have you heard from her?'

John had a mobile that he used sometimes for work, but he didn't really do with phones, so I'd had to walk into town to use the payphone near the shops, dialling the number on the business card the Leeds lawyer had given me outside the courts, along with the rucksack.

It was still morning, and I looked to the shopfronts around the square and the one or two people that were about. Mol was sitting being petted by a passerby, some old lady with a gentle face who purred and coddled and called Mol 'darling', and seemed nice.

'No,' I said. 'Not for a while. Why?'

'Well, you might want to tell her you're OK. We don't want social services sniffing around the caravan, do we? Not while you're on your own. Maybe you should think about going back to school.'

'Did John say that?'

'About your mother? No, but it's sensible, isn't it? Maybe she'll give you some money.'

'Don't need any. I'm all right.'

'Nevertheless, I'll visit you in a couple of days, see that things are as they should be. In the meantime, tell no one your father's away. And no looking in the bag, you understand? Keep your head down and don't cause any trouble. And listen, if a man called Toomey comes around, don't talk to him. He's a Bad Man. Oh,' he added then, sounding sort of embarrassed, 'and John says, watch out for bears, whatever that means. But I suppose you'll know.'

'Beautiful dog, isn't she?' said the old woman, when I put down the phone. She was cupping Mol's face in her hands. 'What is she?'

I still had the lawyer's words rattling loud in my head, but I looked at Mol's pale fur and her grey eyes. 'A retriever maybe? She's a good girl,' I told the lady, not knowing what else to say. I wanted to be away, in case someone I knew recognised me. My school wasn't far away, just half a mile from the shops, and even though I hadn't been there for ages now, someone would still recognise me if they saw me, and I didn't want to be seen. Because no way was I going back there, no matter what the Leeds lawyer said. No matter, school was over for me.

'If you like her, you can have her,' I said to the old woman, trying to make a joke. I felt nervous. That thing the lawyer had said about someone called Toomey made me think I shouldn't be out and about if I didn't need to be.

I didn't like the name, because it made me think of graveyards and dank stone and death. Had John mentioned him before? He'd told me most of the blokes' names but this one didn't mean anything to me.

Toomey.

'No, darling, I can tell she loves you. You keep her,' the old woman said, going along with the joke and nodding to Mol. 'Sweet old girl,' she added, which made me feel sort of sad, because I hadn't even noticed Mol was old. I'd never had a dog before, and she was new to me so I thought she must be new all round. Stupid, really.

'Thank you,' was all I could say, walking away. I'd wanted to make another call, but I felt exposed in the shopping square, so I made off. Mol followed me, and when I looked back a minute later the old woman was still there, but she wasn't smiling any more. Maybe she'd noticed the dirt on my clothes, and the tears in the sleeves of my coat, because she looked sort of worried and about to say something, glancing around for someone to tell, before thinking better of it.

FOUR

'I'LL COME TONIGHT, if John's away.' This was Mam an hour later, after I'd walked down the bypass and found the payphone by the bus stop. 'We could go to the pub and have something hot to eat, if you like. John won't mind. How'd he do in court?'

'Good,' I lied. 'He's to go back in a month's time.'

'So, about tea tonight—'

'No, I'm fine. I just wanted to say hello, that's all. He'll be back at ten,' I said, with another lie – they'd been piling up since she'd answered the call. John was away on business, that was it. Wetherby, buying or selling, I didn't know which. Simple lies were the best, that much I did know – easy to believe. But I hadn't bargained on how I'd feel hearing her voice, and now it was making my guts turn and ache. Because of the nerves there.

'Are you safe?'

'I – I'm fine, yeah.' Guilt, twisting, was it? Or maybe I just missed her like buggery.

My mam, her name's Joanne – Jo to people who know her – but she's Mam to me. The summer he was back from overseas – John, I mean – Mam had been dead nervous. 'Happy nerves,' she'd told me when I asked. But they were nerves that shook through her every day

17

from first in the morning to the last fag at night in the garden, holding herself thin against the rake of the sunshine and thinking things I couldn't fathom. 'What do you suppose he'd like to eat?' she'd ask, staring to the sky. 'We should sort the backroom out, make it like an office for him, to get away from us when he needs to. You know, quiet.' And the next day when we were at the shops: 'What do you think of this one?' with her trying on dresses, pulling them from the racks in shops and this searing love in her face that shone like a real bright light and made her seem drunk to me. So maybe they were still together, after all, or at least she thought so, hoped so. Because that's how she behaved, like a lass in love. 'No big fuss,' she'd say, 'but a celebration. Let's show him we've missed him, eh?'

Every day was like that, her happy and worried and planning, and me going along with it, happy to make her happy. But the thing is, I hadn't missed him, not really. Maybe I'd been too young when he went, and the times he'd spent at home were so rare and filled with a sort of chaos. Happy chaos, like Mam's happy nerves. And her and him going off like sweethearts, like kids, and me watching. And maybe I was jealous, maybe I was, but we'd been fine together, her and me, or so I'd thought.

'Maybe you'll come see me soon. I'm free on Saturday, or Sunday I'll be in the shop.' Mam, she worked in the newsagent's, then at the nursing home the rest of the time. 'Hello?'

'Hello. Yeah,' I said, 'maybe.'

It was me that had called, but now I was talking to her, I wanted out of it. I could hear the nerves there again, but these weren't happy nerves, but something else. Something sadder, and all because of me, I thought, which is a bloody hard thought to hold onto, I can tell you.

'Course,' I said. 'I'm fine. I better get off, but you're all right, aren't you?'

I mean, there's no trouble? *No blokes coming round?* *No men who smell like graveyards standing at your door wanting in?* is what I wanted to ask. But couldn't. And barely after we'd started, it was over again. 'Bye, Mam.'

And done.

Thing about Mam is there's no one better than her, and so why would I up and leave for a stinking van in the woods? There was school, of course, that I hated and that hated me. And there was the change in us all that year he was back, but mainly there was John. She knew it as well as me, the truth of it, I mean. She knew what he needed and what he couldn't stand. When he was bad, when he was lashed with pain and anger, he'd let no one near him but me. It would be me he'd let hold him, me he'd apologise to. Me, and not her, which must have broke her heart, I suppose. What heart there was left unbroken.

I was her son more than his, and so I took on what she'd taken on, whether I liked it or not.

'He's like a pet that wants free,' she'd tell me sometimes, before he came, back when it was her and me and the house was home. Before guns and Toomey and seven kinds of eating mushroom. Back when she had dreams. Sometimes she'd wrap her arms around me at night before bed, like she needed to have something – anything – in her arms or she'd go mad. Her behind me, chin on my shoulder, voice in my ear. 'He can't stand fussing, but let him go wild and he'd starve to death.' It would be a joke between us, because he could hardly make toast, so how was he surviving in the desert? And good job they had a mess there, eh? Mess meaning kitchen, meaning cooks, meaning proper food. Not chaos. The joke was a way of not thinking about the war, of us forgetting.

The happy nerves got worse, closer we got. Then John's flight landed, and it was party time. Mam and me had put out a big sign in the front garden, blue school poster paint on an old pink bedsheet: *WELCOME BACK*. We'd got the neighbours round, and white plastic furniture and a barbecue and balloons. Music playing on a stereo through the open windows of the frontroom, and me and Mam dancing on the grass in our bare feet. Old music – Bob Marley and Bowie and The Jam. Stuff he liked. By midday he still hadn't shown up. Mam got a text to say he had things he needed to sort out, old colleagues to see, desert mates.

Sorry, he'd said. *Soon, though. Love to the lad.*

The burgers and hotdogs got eaten, and the music played on, but me, I was waiting for him, waiting for his silhouette at the end of the street. Dreading it and wanting it at the same time, because by then I'd caught the bug, the excitement and the happy nerves. Mam pulled me back to the party, and later that night when we were packing everything up, she was saying that it was all fine, all of it. He just wanted to check in with his buddies. 'It all takes time,' she said. 'It's a big thing, coming home. We need to be patient.'

The bears and stags John would talk about later weren't even a thing back then. This was before the dreams of wolves underground, before they woke me up clawing at the dirt. My mind was just on school and TV and Mam, and part of me hoped he wouldn't be back at all. Part of me prayed for it, no matter how stupid that seems. Because it's not that I even believe in God. But you pray for all sorts when you're scared. Mam was first in them, me praying for God to keep her safe and make her happy. I'd say these things under my breath at night, while I could hear Mam downstairs, clearing up or setting things in the kitchen for the morning. I prayed that I could make her happy somehow, prayed to be strong. I prayed and I looked out at the stars above the streetlights and I prayed for everything to stay the same, too.

And maybe, I tell myself, maybe I should have prayed harder, or maybe God knows when you don't really believe in Him, sees through the lie, because if He was any sort of god, He would, wouldn't He? Either way, things did change. That's nature. And before I knew it, it was just John and me in the woods. And Mam, she was at home and waiting for us. And that's how it stayed for a while.

Woods were always his home, I think. Not a house. Sometimes it felt like he'd been born in the ferns, with moss as his bed. He'd often talk about how he'd lived alone for months in a forest in Europe, before he came back, before we even knew he was coming home. He was out the army then, working contract work. Anyway, in this forest, he said, they still had prehistoric creatures, bears larger than any bear you've seen and bison the size of houses. 'Not like the American bison,' he'd say, smiling and shaking his head like the idea itself was stupid. 'These were taller, with longer horns.'

I didn't believe him, but he had a photograph, which I still have now. It's blurry, the photo, and the bison is half hidden by the trees, but it is pretty big, and black and ancient-looking. He'd show me the photo every now and then when he'd talk about what things were like before everything went to shit, as he'd call it. I'm not sure if he meant the world or his life.

He'd never let me hold the photograph or touch it when he was alive. Some things were sort of sacred to him, like the photo of his grandfather, and the bison and the letters from Mam he kept bundled together that we found after, when it was over.

That March when it all ended, though, he'd slap his hand against the sunlit ground that was still damp from winter, and say, 'And there are the same creatures under here. There were bears and wolves and stags as tall as oak in this country, too. We had all sorts of animals. This is an ancient land, older than anyone knows. This bloke, William Blake, knew that. He painted pictures and wrote poems, did Blake, and he saw what was coming and what had been. And they'll come back, you'll see. They're not gone for ever. The world is just sleeping, and those beasts are asleep with it, but one day they'll climb out of the forest and things will get back to how it should be. You'll see,' he'd say, like it wouldn't be long. 'You'll see.'

FIVE

THE MORNING IT happened, the morning I met Sophie, I hadn't bothered looking at the time. But when I woke it must have been real early because when I went out to pee it was still night-dark, so I could see the little light right off in the distance where there shouldn't have been a light. I thought it might be a star at first, or a planet. Which was funny, thinking back.

I didn't know then, of course, that it was Sophie out there. How could I?

The dreams had woken me, of course. They'd been coming every night now, dreams of animals in the night, amongst the trees. They weren't always scary, but sometimes I'd wake up thinking something was in the van with me, just standing there looking at me. Yellow eyes in the black, sharp as glass.

This was the morning after the Leeds lawyer had been the first time, come to check things over and hand me fifty quid in tens in a brown envelope. 'John's money,' he made sure to tell me, 'not mine. Should last you till he's back. Has Toomey been here?'

I told him no one had, which was true enough.

'Call me if he does.'

I knew the fields at night.

Sometimes when me and John were out we'd see the barn owl flying all ghostly and quiet. And John would tell me how in the past some thought the white owl was good luck and others thought it was bad, and if you were sick and the owl flew past your window, you knew that soon you'd die. He'd point out the trails in the flattened grass where the roe deer would go, and sometimes we'd see a badger and its pups on the east-facing slope of the quarry where the mechanical diggers never went. We'd walk a lot at night, because John was rubbish at sleeping. Sometimes he'd take me across to the train tracks, and we'd follow the line to the edge of town where the mansions were, the ones with swimming pools and garages that were bigger than houses, and houses bigger than schools. Football players would live here, and businessmen. You could watch them from the cuttings if you wanted, because rich people keep their lights on all night, even in the garages and swimming pools. We'd look through the big windows, to the shimmer of blue water cast against the whitewashed walls, and we'd laugh sometimes at the barmy things people get up to. But later John would become fired up and talk all the way home about how they've got it stitched up, and no matter how poor a country gets the rich don't get touched. 'And where's the trick in that? What's the secret, because it isn't coincidence,' he'd say. He had this idea that rich people were the real anarchists, that they liked chaos on their terms, because there's profit in chaos. It all tied in with how things Were instead of how they Seemed. 'If you know what to bet on, a smart man can make a lot of money out of people getting poor,' he said. 'It's like a war. Them that know stand on the sidelines, betting big on the outcome, and them that don't, they're the ones that get killed or have their legs blown off or go mad, and if they're lucky they get a medal for it to show their kids after.'

Every time we went to the big houses it would just get him angry, so I never got why he wanted to keep going all the time. It was only when he was arrested that I found out that he'd been scouting for places to rob. That's what the coppers told me anyway, and John never said he never, so it had to be true. Despite the stuff he'd say about good men and doing right. He was a hypocrite, then, which was funny, because John hated hypocrites. Which goes to show that men don't make sense, none of them. That's what I think.

'Who are you?'

The voice in the dark made me jump. I still had pictures of bad men who smelled of graves in my head. I didn't even get that it was a girl's voice straight away, that's how scared I was. The torchlight in my face didn't help, either.

'Get that thing off me.'

'Oh, sorry – wait.' The light bounced against the ground, flickered as she fumbled with the switch. 'Here,' she said, as the torch blinked off. 'Sorry, I didn't mean to frighten you.'

'I'm not frightened,' I said, but my voice told the story, I couldn't help it. 'You don't just shove a light in someone's face.'

'Sorry,' she said again.

'What are you doing in the woods anyway?' I said, trying to sound more angry than scared. I didn't know that right then her head was as full of stars as mine was full of villains.

'Jupiter,' she said, like that answered any questions I had, rather than just being nonsense. I stared at her, thinking she might be barmy, while she pointed over my shoulder to the sky. And when I still didn't catch on, she said, 'I suppose you'd call it stargazing. You know, the planets. Are you from the farm?'

'What farm?'

The balls of light from the torch were still flashing in my eyes, big as sparrows, but I could see her now, not far away. She was tall and thin and her hair was tied up under a woolly hat. 'I can't remember his name. Mr Derry or something. He's the farmer. We're camping in his field.'

'Derby,' I said, correcting her. 'Yeah, I know him.'

Derby was a fat man with a red face, and him and John had a deal about the caravan and us living in the woods. Derby owned all the farmland around here, but he wasn't one of those lot that John hated. Not that John liked him, he didn't. 'But at least he works for a living,' John said. 'A bloke who farms and grows things isn't a Parasite.' He was big on Parasites, John. He had this postcard of one of William Blake's paintings. Blake was one of the poets John liked, and he liked his pictures, too, and he pinned this postcard head-high to the corkboard on the cupboard next to the sink. A picture called *The Flea*. So you'd think it'd be a picture of a flea, like a dog flea or something, wouldn't you? But it's not a flea at all, just this fella that looks like he's out of a monster film, some demon or vampire that'll

27

eat you if he finds you. You'll know it when you see it, and you won't forget it, I can tell you. It's a real horror show. To John, the world had too many fleas, too many Parasites feeding off us, trying to make us hate, pitting us against ourselves. It was Parasites that sent him to war, he said, and them that'll start the next one and blame foreigners or Muslims or Jews or anybody but themselves.

'Do you live here?' This was the girl again. I could see her breath as she spoke, dim clouds lit up by that tiny light in the distance that wasn't there usually. She noticed I was looking at it, and turned and said, 'We're at the edge of the field. That's our campervan. We've hired it.' She nodded to the light, a blue lamp on the far side of the field, so far it winked in the night like a star.

'Beautiful, isn't it?' she said. 'The night, I mean.' She'd turned her face to the sky, and watching her I felt the ground tilt a bit beneath my feet. A chill went over me, and I never usually felt the cold.

'Right,' I said.

She was like that for what felt like a minute, and me not breathing, just watching her. And then without another word she crouched down and gave Mol a stroke on her nose. 'I'm Sophie,' she said.

I didn't know if she was telling me or the dog.

'I'm back there in the trees,' I said. 'We've got a caravan. We live there.'

She nodded without getting up or looking at me, and I just stood, sort of feeling at a loose end while she and Mol got to know each other. 'So, you from Leeds?' I asked.

'No, Wales.'

'Wales? You don't have an accent or anything.' Her voice was posh, she could have come from anywhere. I'd never been to Wales, but once John had had an idea to live there. He said there was a place, just small, where you could live off-grid. No internet, no mobile phone signal, nothing but quiet and nature and being left alone to live your life. 'Do you have internet?' I asked.

'At the campervan?' the girl – Sophie – said, looking up at me, confused.

'No, in Wales.' I felt stupid as soon as I said it, because it's a stupid thing to ask, I get that. But it's one of those daft things you come out with when you've got nothing to say, and anyway it was too late to take it back now. 'It's just John said there's a place in Wales where you can live with no one knowing.'

'Oh,' she said, uncertain, looking at Mol, then back at me.

I shuffled my feet a bit, wishing I was dead.

But Sophie just kept stroking Mol's head, and then she said: 'Well, we're moving to live here soon. Not far. That's why we came, because Dad thought we should get to know the place. It's what we're doing for the next week or so – touring about.'

'So, you're skiving off school, like me,' I said, because I knew half term had long passed, and Easter was still way off.

'Sort of,' Sophie answered, smiling. 'We told the school, though. Dad's changing jobs and, well, my folks are going through some things right now. It's complicated, you know? Money problems.'

I nodded. I knew complicated all right.

Sophie got to her feet and stared at me. Her eyes were colourless in the low morning light, but there were pale sparks in them, grey and flickering. 'Who's John?' she said.

'He's my dad.'

Neither of us said anything for a bit then. We stood there and watched our breath cloud in the air between us, and listened to the morning birds that had begun to sing round about – blackbirds first, and then wrens, robins, thrushes coming later, when the first light appears. There's an order to it all, and I wanted to tell her that. I wanted to tell her how some birds get up before the others, and it changed depending on the month, but no matter when it was, the blackbird was always first because he always had a lot to say, and liked the sound of his own voice.

I could just about see the rest of her face now. It was pretty. She was about my age, I thought. Same height, or maybe a bit taller.

'Well, I should go,' Sophie said. 'We're hiking today, but I'll be back later, before supper, if you're around.'

Maybe I nodded. I can't remember now. But I didn't reply, I know that much. I just watched her walk away, not knowing what had just happened or whether it meant nothing or something. And then when she was at the edge of the field, the winking blue light drawing her side like a piece of chalk, she stopped and turned and waved, but real casual, like she'd almost forgotten I was there.

And I waved back.

SIX

I WENT BACK TO bed and slept late that morning. But it was broken sleep, filled with dreamed noises outside, a big black bear circling the caravan, sniffing the air. I imagined I could hear a bison cropping the young grass on the sandbar in the stream, and further on something smaller snuffling, not much bigger than a pig. In my dream I couldn't turn, couldn't see what it was, but I knew. Wolves. Those yellow eyes in the dark, watchful and rich as butter, and their coats thick down to their bones, frost-covered. Two or more of them, and in my dreams they never hurt me, but I could smell the dirt on them, the centuries falling off their shoulders like so much rust. Ancient.

Sometimes I'd dream I was running with them, the wolves, and I was one of them, because that's what John said we were once. He said there were bears and there were wolves, and the difference was bears hunted alone and wolves stayed together, and we were wolves, and that's what made us strong. And sometimes there'd be a lone wolf, one time in a hundred, and he was the one you had to look out for, because he was danger.

When I got up I had to check through the window, just to see if there really were wolves and bison there, even though I knew it had all been in my head.

Dreams are like that, real enough so you wake up crying or laughing sometimes. John had some awful dreams that made him scream and shake, and more than once I'd had to hold him down because he'd start to thrash out, and if he'd caught me in the cramped caravan with a stray hand maybe he would have bust my head open.

He had once. Caught me a good one, given me a shiner so bad I'd had to avoid Mam for nearly two weeks while it went down, so she wouldn't see it. It wasn't on purpose, though, and in the morning when he'd looked at what he'd done in his sleep, he'd near collapsed on the floor of the van, like a kid. Blubbing. Proper blubbing, until I calmed him down and told him over and over that it was all right, that I didn't blame him. That I loved him. But that night before bed he asked me to zip him up in his sleeping bag and put the blue twine around, to keep his arms at his side, in case it happened again. Which I did.

But late in the night, what I'd do was loosen off the twine and I'd sit and watch him sleep, see his legs kick and his jaw tense, and I'd keep a watch over him, because he was a bigger danger to himself than to me, only I don't think he ever saw that.

I'd sit and watch and I'd wait there until the nightmares ended, and sometimes I'd get near enough to push the hair from his face, because when he dreamed, he'd sweat like he was still in the desert, still under fire. His hair would be wet through, see, but then it would be over and I knew he was sleeping properly, because he'd snore. And that's when I'd sit out on the van steps and I'd look at the stream in the moonlight and thank God I'd never have to be called up to fight.

Dogs dream, too.

I didn't know that before I met Mol. That morning after Sophie came, Mol was on the blanket in the corner, chasing rabbits in her sleep, but I didn't notice straight away because now I was proper awake and my heart was hammering on account of something I'd just remembered from the dream. Something that wasn't wolves and bears, but scarier: the noise of footsteps in the stream, men's boots. And now I was thinking about the rucksack and the thing inside, and the man named Toomey. Because somehow I knew Toomey and the gun were all mixed up with the Job John would talk about.

I never liked thinking about the Job, because even though I didn't know what it was, I knew it couldn't be good. He'd talked about it in February almost as much as he talked about Gold and Stars.

'You'll see, once the Job's over, things will be different. We'll go to Scotland, buy a croft, away from people. Just you and me.'

'Is a croft like a house?'

'Yeah, just like that.'

'Can Mam come?'

'If she wants. Would you want her to?'

'Course.'

'Then, yeah, she can come. And we can get some goats, because they're just as good as sheep, but tougher. Chickens, too. I'll teach you how to fillet a fish.'

'It's not like skinning rabbits?'

'No, much easier,' John said. 'Like peeling a ripe pear.'

Skinning rabbits was my worst thing in the woods. They were dead when it was time, so it wasn't that I felt too bad hurting them, not really. But because they were slippery after you pulled away the fur they had a hard time staying in your hand. First time I tried, the greasy thing squirmed out of my fingers and onto the fire and I heard John sigh, disappointed. And I never wanted to try again, and he didn't force me to.

I couldn't see how fish would be easier, but he said they were so I tried to believe it.

'Will you have to go away for the Job?' I asked. I knew there were no jobs around here, not big ones that would give us the money to move to Scotland. The only job I knew about was the army and what would I do if he joined up again? Would he want me to be a soldier, too? Because I didn't want to. Not that I was a coward, I'm not. But I'm not brave, either, and the things he'd told me he'd witnessed hadn't left my head, and when I heard him moan in the night I knew some of the pictures he was seeing by what he'd said. The one with the fountains of fire in the sand, and the man vanishing in the red dust, and the boy – the boy was the worst, and I didn't want to see them first hand, none of them, no way. 'Will you?' I said.

'Not *away* away,' he told me. 'Anyway, it might be a long way off, so don't worry yourself,' he added, ending the discussion.

This was the week before he was arrested and the Job still seemed like it might never happen, just one of John's daydreams. We were sat outside, I remember, both staring at the fire. Some nights while it got darker I'd watch his profile against the flames and he'd get out the photo of his grandfather. A strong man with the name of Amos, who'd once been a champion boxer. John said it like he was proud, although I knew he hated his grandfather because he'd told me that, too, on the only time I'd seen him drunk. It was after he'd come back from the desert on leave and him and Mam had had a fight, a bad one, with both of them saying the worst things, and he'd had a bottle of whisky, and he'd drunk the whole thing and then broke a door. He'd shouted at me about how his grandfather would clout him, just for looking at him funny, and when he'd gone at the door Mam had threatened to call the police but she never that time, because she loved him, like me. And she was sad for him, but when she said she hated him she meant it, and I did, too. Not that it lasted with either of us, the hate. It never did. But while it was there it was hot as fire, and real.

John had boxed when he was my age, that's the story. They'd called him Iron John at the gym, not because he had a strong punch but because when he got hit he just kept standing up and refused to drop. 'Too proud for my own good, they told me. And it hasn't changed much since,' he'd say, with a laugh. If Mam was there when he said it, she'd laugh, too, but in a sad way that I couldn't work out back then. Sad, like it was a memory of something lost.

'How long have you been here?' This was Sophie, that evening. I'd found her standing with her face tilted up to the sky as the clouds began to clear, revealing the first stars.

'Since the end of last summer.'

Mol nuzzled her hand, and Sophie went to pet her.

'You had Christmas in the woods?' She smiled when she asked it, then turned back to the stars, calm as you like. 'That must have been really special.' Funny how some people are easy to talk to. Sophie was like that, and she didn't ask the stuff folk banged on about real quick usually, like why wasn't I in school, and didn't I need a proper place to live? She had a way of making me feel normal, which is a good trick, and rare, I'll tell you that much.

'There was snow all January,' I said, grinning. 'Up to our knees. Ice on the windows. We built a fire every day with wood we'd stored on a palette to keep it off the ground. Kept it dry with a tarpaulin.' I never told her about how the wood was still a bugger to light, and how I'd wake up every morning shaking, and thinking my fingers would drop off with frostbite. Somehow, talking to her I just remembered the good things. Then she told me about her and her family, and how they were struggling with stuff. How Sophie was worried they'd divorce maybe. All because of some money problems, she said. Although, they sounded like money problems my mam would have been glad to have. The move would be a fresh start,

Sophie said. And me, I was thinking how it just went to show that there are different kinds of people, and they all have their problems. She smiled when she talked about it, trying to hide the worry and the fear, I suppose. And after, when it was time for her to go and I was on my own again in the trees, I realised I'd forgotten a lot of the bad of that last winter in the woods – the mud and cold and the no sleeping, and the fear. Because I had been afraid sometimes. Not that I told John, not ever. Because he didn't put up with fear, didn't value it. His dad didn't put up with it before him, and I wasn't supposed to, either.

Just, I wasn't very good at not feeling fear. Not like John. And I couldn't smile about it, like Sophie. So maybe I was just too soft, I thought.

Later that night, as I watched Mol kick her legs in her sleep, I pictured John in his cell and I thought of that grandfather of his, with the blond hair and the moustache and the fists liked balled rock, and I wanted to be hard, too, and a fighter like them. I was sick of being scared all the time.

It was a week later that the Bad Man came.

SEVEN

I'D BEEN OUT to Armley, out to the gaol. I'd taken John cigarettes and a book he liked. The cigarettes were because I'd heard you could get money for them in gaol. I'd gone to four different shops in town before one of them served me, this skinny bloke not much older than me who looked embarrassed as I handed over the money. It cost me as much as we'd spend on two weeks' shopping, and when I got to the gaol John didn't seem interested in them, and anyway the guards took them away from me and I still don't know if he got to sell them to the other prisoners.

The book was better, and made him smile. It was something he'd read over and over, which seemed weird to me, because I couldn't see the point of reading anything more than once. It was by the man called Blake, who John said was a genius, and saw things as they Were instead of how they Seemed, which I didn't get at the time, but I do now. He meant the way people see things isn't always the truth, but just what they want to see. Or what they're taught to see, even, because we don't always have a choice, even when we're grown up.

The book wasn't a proper story, but poems, and at night John would read them out to me, kind of like a prayer. I probably know half of them off by heart, even though I'd never looked at the book back then.

'You eating? You look skinny,' John said, when I sat down at the little table and chair that reminded me of school. There were rows of them, and other men like John were sitting waiting for people to arrive, and looking bored. 'You're keeping all right, yeah?' he added, but he wasn't worried, he was just talking. He'd rolled up the cuffs of the shirt he had on, and I could see the hairs on his arms. John's hands were large and covered in thick blond hair. 'Has Alan been in touch? He said he'd bring you some cash this week.'

I said he had, and then John turned the book over in his hands for a few minutes, smiling and telling me, 'There aren't enough books in here, that's the problem. Give men something to occupy their minds and they won't need to rob and fight and hate.'

I thought about that and saw it was true, sort of. I wanted to say so, but it didn't explain why John robbed houses, because he read plenty, more books than I could count. And the truth is he robbed houses anyway. The coppers were right about that. Not many, mind, but one robbed house is still a robbed house, isn't it? I wanted to ask him why if reading was so important, it hadn't stopped him, but I said nothing, because you couldn't argue with him sometimes. He'd do things his way and that was that.

'What happens here?' I asked, looking around the prison room and trying not to catch anyone's eye.

He smiled a bit and said, 'Same as outside, but without the woods and the work and the fresh air and the van, and you.'

Which I didn't understand, because apart from those things, John did nothing but sleep and think. The woods and the work were all he had.

'You seen anyone lately? You're not lonely, are you?'

I smiled when he said it, because I was thinking of Sophie, and I was going to tell him how we'd met, and how I'd seen her three times now, and how she'd taught me to find the constellation of Leo in the night sky, and how it doesn't look like a lion at all, but a horse.

Only, I didn't tell him. I didn't tell him how her and her parents had been at the coast for the last few days, but they'd be back tonight. Or how I'd got a book on astrology out of the library, so I could learn what she knew. Because that's what she did, and it's why she was there in the field that first time – to see the stars, I mean. It's what she loved. I didn't tell him how I'd taught myself to say 'Good morning' in Welsh, so I could surprise her with it when I saw her next.

'No, nobody,' I said. 'Just the lawyer.'

I never told him how her and her folks would be moving to Ainsley Heath in about a week, either – which wasn't far, just a thirty-minute bus ride between me and her.

Looking back, I suppose I'd wanted her to myself, like I'd wanted Mol to myself. Mine, a secret, something I could keep away from the world for a bit.

We talked about other stuff, me and John, then he told me to keep hold of the rucksack, but not to worry about it too much. 'You're a worrier,' he said, 'but I don't want you worrying about me in here, all right? I'm fine. It's easier than the army and it's got a better bed than the one in the caravan.' He grinned, and I believed him.

'Maybe I should rob a house, and then I can get a decent bed, too,' I said. It was a joke and not a joke at the same time, because I was still thinking about what he'd said about robbing and books and men not fighting.

'Don't you ever rob a house, you got that?' he said, proper angry. 'You're never to do anything I do, not ever. Promise me.'

'All right,' I said, but I was annoyed, because he knew it was a joke and I didn't see why he had to get upset with me about it.

'Promise me,' he repeated, loud enough for everyone to hear.

'*All right*,' I said, 'I promise.' I caught the bloke at the next table smirking at me, and I suppose I must have blushed, because John reached over and squeezed my hand.

'It's important, that's all,' he said, looking less annoyed now. 'I don't want you ending up in here. It's all right for me, but not for you. You get it, don't you?'

'Yeah, yeah,' I said, pulling my hand away, embarrassed. 'I get it.'

'Good lad.'

He'd shaved while he'd been inside, and he looked different, younger. I liked how he looked, and I thought Mam would like it, too, but I wasn't going to tell him because I was pissed off with him now.

'Who's Toomey?' I asked, after a minute.

John stared at me, a flicker of anger returning to his eyes. 'Alan been talking to you?'

I nodded.

Seconds passed.

'He's just a man,' John said, at last. 'That's all. He runs some businesses in town.'

'Do I know him?' I'd been going over in my mind all the blokes who'd come by the caravan in their flash cars. They were Jaguars and Mercedes mostly, and sometimes a big, black Range Rover that looked like it had just come out of the car wash, and was always careful not to park too close to the muddy run-off by the stream.

'Why would you know him?' John said, smiling like it wasn't worth either of us even talking about. 'Listen, when you see Alan next, I want you to do something for me. Under the van there's a packet of money in a lunchbox. I want you to give it to him. You don't have to say what it is, just hand it over and he'll be on his way, all right?'

'But I thought he was giving us money?'

'It's different money, like a swap, yeah? Do you understand?'

'All right.'

'You don't have to count it, just hand it over. Alan knows what it is.' I had a million questions to ask, but I couldn't think of the important one, not then. It kept slipping away every time I tried to catch it, slick as a skinned rabbit. My head was filled with money and flash cars and books, and the stuffy smell of the gaol. I wanted to go, and I wanted John to come back to the woods with me, and not stay here any longer with the other blokes and their bored faces and cocky smiles.

'And don't give Toomey a thought,' John said, as the buzzer went for the end of visiting time and I was told to go wait at the door. 'He won't come near you. Leave him to me.'

And I would have done, too, but when I was making my way through the woods that afternoon, past the quarry, and down the stream, I saw something black and gleaming through the trees, big as a bull. It was the Range Rover. And I knew all at once who'd be waiting for me at the caravan.

EIGHT

'THIS DOG LIKES me,' he said, as I made my way up to the door. He'd got himself right at home in the caravan, and was sitting at the little fold-out table where we'd eat and John would read. Mol was sitting at the man's feet, staring at nothing much. His hand was at her neck, sort of kneading her fur. 'She yours? Didn't know your old man likes dogs.'

'How'd you get in?' I asked, looking at the door to see if it had been broken. When we'd moved in, John had screwed a latch on it, with a padlock, and the padlock was open now and on the table next to the man's elbow. I stood and stared at it and tried not to look surprised, tried not to look too bothered by having this bloke here, this man.

'These vans are pretty flimsy, aren't they? Not the sort of place to hide your valuables, but John doesn't go for many luxuries, does he? Likes the simple life. I suppose living out of a tent and marching over a desert does that to you. Not that I haven't tried to persuade him to get a house, especially as he's got a kid with him now. I've got plenty of properties he could rent at a good price if you ever want to look one over, nice semis with gardens, proper family homes. Friends help friends out, don't they?' He grabbed Mol's neck and squeezed, trying to make it look affectionate. But it was too rough, and his grin was too wide.

He had a black suit on, the man. Shiny, with shiny black shoes with tassles, and no socks. And he was tanned, liked he'd just come back from holidays. John would have said he was a preener, an old peacock.

'Come here, girl,' I said, slapping my hand against my leg. Mol blinked up at me, but didn't move straight away. The man smiled. 'Here, Mol!' I said, louder.

She got up then and padded towards me. I went to the sink and poured some water into a bowl from the glass bottles we kept in the corner for drinking. I put the bowl on the floor and watched as Mol nosed it, looked up at me and then began to drink.

'You're good with her,' the man said. 'Could I have some of that water?'

It was cramped in the van, and he had his knees spread, his tanned ankles showing beneath his trouser legs. I had to move past him to get to the cups. I got John's thick china mug and poured some water in it and gave it to the man. 'How do you know John?' I asked. It was the question I'd wanted to ask at Armley, but I hadn't been able to get the words out or my thoughts straight then.

'Him and me are friends,' the man said, taking a sip of water.

'But how?'

'Your old man provided some services for me, let's call it that. We'll be working on something else soon, all being well. Nice little job, good rewards.'

He put the mug down on the table and frowned at me till his forehead was all lines and his eyes were squeezed together tight. Like he had a real bad headache all of a sudden.

'You *are* John Hill's lad, aren't you?'

'Course. He's my dad.'

'Just, you're too quiet. I expected someone louder. John's got a mouth on him, hasn't he? Doesn't mind throwing his weight around.'

'I suppose.'

'Thought you'd be a lot like him, but you're not. Thought I might have had trouble with you, but I can see you and me won't have any trouble, will we?'

I didn't like the way he sat there at our table and how comfy he seemed, and I didn't like the way he looked at me, like everything was funny to him.

'I'm not supposed to talk to you,' I said.

'No? Why's that?'

I shrugged.

I knew you can't tell a Bad Man that he's a Bad Man. They don't like it. It's like telling a bully he's a bully, even though you both know it, and he's proud of it in a sort of way. But you just can't say it, like it's a rule. There'd been a bully at school, kid called Otley, and he was one of the reasons I didn't mind when John told me I should leave to live with him, and he'd teach me what the teachers never would. John had a thing about schools, said they stopped a kid from thinking for himself, put us all in boxes that we'd never get out of if we weren't careful. They'd put him in a box, he said, and the army had put him in another one, and now no one else would put him in a box, not even the council, although they kept trying.

'Is Mam in a box?' I'd asked.

'Sort of,' he'd said. 'But she can cope with it, she's strong like that. And I can't. Some of us are better at being in boxes than others.'

I understood that, because Otley had tried to keep me in a box, and I hadn't coped with it. Every day he'd come over, nick my money and give me a clout. I'd tell him to pack it in, but that just made it worse. Bullies, they want you to fight back, but they hate it when you do. They want you to cry, but if you do cry it just gets worse. You can't please them, is what it is, so you have to keep your mouth shut, just in case.

'Has John told you about me?' the man asked.

'No.'

'Then how come you can't talk to me? I'm friendly enough, aren't I? Have I done anything to give you reason not to like me?'

'No.'

'Well, everything's all right then, isn't it?' He wasn't even looking at me now. He was knocking the dog hair from his trousers with his hand. Wetting his fingers and picking off a bit of muck here and there. 'Me and your old man had a deal, did you know that? I helped him out of a spot. It's why I'm here. He wanted me to check in on you, see you weren't getting into any trouble.' He looked up at me, and he wasn't smiling any more. 'So I'm standing in for him, really. While he's not here, I'm sort of your dad.'

'I've got the lawyer for that,' I said.

'Alan?'

I didn't know he knew the lawyer's name, and he saw it and liked that I hadn't known, and looked even more smug.

'Alan's OK, but he's not too bright. These blokes who've been to university think they know stuff, but they're not like your dad and me. They know books and laws and they're good at filling in a form, but they can't understand the sort of business your dad and me do. They haven't got the belly for it.'

'What sort of business is that?'

'He hasn't told you?'

I shook my head, and he looked at me and stopped smiling.

'We're in the security business, him and me. We secure loyalty, mostly.' He watched my face, as though he expected me to say something, and when I didn't, he asked, 'So, how many men do you think he killed out there?' He meant the desert and the war.

I didn't know what that had to do with anything, so I said, 'Don't know.'

'Doesn't he talk about it?'

'No.'

'You've never asked him?'

'No.'

'If it was me I'd be telling everyone I knew. I'd brag about it. Man who can take someone's life like that, well, it's impressive, isn't it?'

'He's not a bragger, though.'

Thing is, John never talked about killing anyone, not even when he'd first come back. Not even with Mam. That's what a lot of the arguments were about, because he wouldn't talk to her. He'd only tell us that it hadn't been good out there, and they were just waiting a lot of the time, baking in the heat in their boots and their helmets, and when they weren't waiting they were being shot at or blown up. But most of the time it was waiting, and that whoever said it was a war was wrong.

'Your old man's got a lot of skills, but his problem is the skills he has don't help getting work in an office or a pub or a shop. Men like him are good fighting in wars, but peace isn't too kind to them, is it? That's why he had to come to me, because I appreciate what he can do. Maybe he'll teach you, when you're old enough.' He looked at me and narrowed his eyes, and I thought he was going to give me one of those smug grins again, but he didn't. 'Maybe he's already teaching you, eh?'

I let him think what he wanted, and just stood there.

'Anyway,' he said, getting up. He picked up the mug and finished the water. 'I can tell him that you're all right here, can I? Safe and sound. And now you and me have met, things can go nice and smooth between us all.' He moved past me to the door, bending his head down, because the caravan ceiling was low, and he was tall, taller than John, even. 'I'll see you again, lad,' he said.

He climbed down out of the caravan, and stepped gingerly across the mud, so he wouldn't muck up his polished shoes, over to the sandbar and then across the rest of the stream and then over and up to where the Range Rover was parked. And he didn't turn around or say goodbye, just got in and reversed up the hill, to the lane, where I heard the Range Rover accelerate back towards town. And even then I knew I'd see him again, I just didn't know that when I did, it would be the end of everything. The end of John and me, and Gold and Stars. And it would be soon.

NINE

WHEN HE WAS gone I felt sort of numb, like I'd been holding myself stiff all the time he'd been there. There was something about Toomey that made you nervous even when he was smiling. Especially when he was smiling. I got in a panic, thinking why had he come, and remembered what John had said about the money. So I ran straight out of the caravan and to the back.

I pulled away the lean-to screens we'd made for the seeding trays where we grew veg and stuff, and got down on my hands and knees and crawled right under the van, as far as I could. Breathing hard.

There was a steel tool box half dug into the ground. The lid was locked with a little key that John had given me, and I unlocked it and shoved my hands in quick, and pulled out what was inside. A plastic lunchbox as big as a brick, and heavy with money.

So Toomey hadn't found it then, if that's what he was after. It was safe and the smug sod had wasted his trip, I thought. I would have smiled about it if I hadn't been so scared.

Mol had come out to see what the fuss was about. She was trying to pull herself beneath the caravan, but her hips were too stiff and the caravan was too low.

'Get lost, Mol. Go!'

She shuffled away while I pulled myself out of the mud. There was mud on my jeans and my hands, and my boots and socks were soaked through. I was cold, and felt stupid and scared. I carried the lunchbox with the money inside the caravan and locked the door with the padlock, and bolted the door, too, and closed the curtains in the van.

It was ages until I thought about the rucksack. Which, if you think about it, should have been the first thing on my mind, not the last. And that's how stupid I was back then. But when I went to the bedroom and pulled the rucksack out from beneath John's mattress, and unzipped it, the gun was there. A big one. Like a shotgun, but with the barrels cut right down. It smelled funny, and there was this cloth it was wrapped in that was soft with oil. And a plastic bag tied around the heavy stock and trigger with an elastic band.

Looking at it sort of made me dizzy, and I had a sick feeling in my stomach. I held the gun in my hands and felt how heavy it was, and wondered if it had ever shot anyone. I'd never seen one before, only on telly. I sniffed the barrels to see if it had been fired, but I didn't know what gunpowder or shot or bullets or whatever smelled like, but it smelled bitter anyway.

There was plenty I didn't know. I didn't know what John was supposed to do with the gun or whether Toomey was behind it being here, because who else did John know that would give him a shotgun? And I didn't know what the lawyer man was coming around for, but it wasn't just to see if I was doing all right, I knew that much. And none of it helped me sleep that night or look forward to the next day.

So, after shoving everything back under the mattress, and after lying awake for hours, I got up and took Mol out to the fields where she could try to sniff out a hare, although she was no better than me at chasing them.

TEN

THE WOLVES CAME again early the next morning, bright and ghostly against the ground, sniffing me out. It was still dark when I woke, shaking, and saw eyes in the shadows of the van, cold as nails. Toomey's eyes. So cold I had to climb up out of the bed and pull on my jeans and walk out and sit by the stream, until my heart slowed. I thought Mol might come up beside me, but she was still tired from last night's walk, so I went to the field alone.

'Don't you ever sleep?'

Sophie was at the corner, the pale wine-coloured grass up to the knees of her jeans, grinning face ruddy with cold. I hadn't seen her for almost a week, and every day I'd been looking forward to this. But now the moment was here I couldn't speak. I'd forgotten all about saying 'Good morning' to her in Welsh. I was frozen there, my head still full of Toomey.

'You OK?' she asked. She'd been looking at the night sky, and I thought I could still see a bit of the starshine in her eyes, mixed with worry.

'Yeah, course,' I said. Even though I'd known all along she'd be back today, I was surprised to see her. And I looked at myself, to see what she saw. There was no need for a torch because the moon was still out and full, lighting up the field, blue. Lighting up the sky. This time of morning was a race, I thought, between the moon and the sun, and the sun always won. Already the horizon was cast cold with the coming day, growing every second, slow and steady and unstoppable.

I hadn't thought to put my coat on, and my jumper had holes in it, steam coming off my back like it was lit by a match, proper hot. It was the fear that had made me hot, always did. Toomey and his words was the cause. My hands, though, they were white and my nose was running so I must have looked like I was in a fever and real sick.

Sick enough for Sophie to ask: 'Are you ill?'

'No, I'm all right.' I wiped the back of my hand across my face. 'I missed you,' I said. 'It's nice you're back.'

Sophie took a step towards me. 'Sorry. If you'd been looking for me, I mean. Had you?'

'No, it's not that. Just—' I didn't finish the sentence, my mind was somewhere else, with guns and gaols and lunchboxes full of money. And I had missed her, course I had, more than she could imagine.

'You want some tea?' I asked. 'It's nettle, not proper tea. And no sugar. But it'll be hot.'

She nodded, and we walked back into the trees, and once we were at the van I lit the paraffin stove and set the kettle, and we sat apart in silence until the kettle whistled and then I poured us two mugs and Sophie said thank you.

The first blackbird of the morning sang on a rock in the stream, the male. There was a nest nearby. I'd kept my eye on it for a couple of weeks now. I'd never known a blackbird nest built on the ground before. It was under a holly bush, and I'd seen three eggs in there, a blue-green colour, best colour you could imagine, like gems or something. I wondered if Sophie would want to see it. I meant to ask her, but something stopped me. Fear, I suppose. The happy nerves Mam talked about.

'I'm adopted,' Sophie said suddenly, when we'd been sat there for a bit.

I imagine my face was a picture, or maybe I'd learned from Mam not to show surprise any more. I tried to find something to say, just anything to fill the silence, but then Sophie said, 'I mean, I've always known, from being little. A relative couldn't look after me, and so Mum and Dad took me in. It's a long story, complicated,' she said, sounding suddenly shy. 'Anyway, once I ran away from home, years ago, after an argument about how they weren't my real parents. Kids' stuff. I thought if I could get to St David's, I could get a job in a café and live there and everything would be fine. St David's is a town that I like, in Wales.'

I nodded, but the place might as well have been Timbuktu. I'd only ever known Yorkshire, and a small corner of it.

Sophie carried on. 'It would be a nice café that served ice cream all day, and I'd call it Sophie's Place. But I never thought about the fact that I was ten and maybe nobody would want a ten-year-old running a café.' She smiled, a really nice smile, taking the mick out of herself to make some kind of point I couldn't grasp. I noticed her face was flushed with the heat of the tea. Her nose was pink. Her eyes the colour of blackbird eggs.

'Have you run away?' she asked, serious now. And now I saw the point, saw what she was trying, gently, to do. 'If you have, you've done better than me.' She nodded to the van. 'I lasted two hours before I had to find my way back home, with my tail between my legs.'

'I'm just waiting for my—' I stopped. 'I'm waiting for John to come back, like I said.'

'And he's away on business, right? He's not the one with the Range Rover, is he? The one that was here yesterday?'

She wasn't being nosy, just talking. But I didn't like it, I never liked talking about John to people. So I got to my feet and picked the postcard of *The Flea* from the corkboard and handed it to her. 'You seen that?' I asked. 'William Blake – he's one of my favourites.'

Sophie looked at the card. 'He wrote the poem about the tiger, didn't he? *Tyger Tyger, burning bright.*'

'That's right.'

In the forests of the night—

'Why do you like him?'

I didn't know how to answer straight away. I'd never thought to ask myself why. 'I like his pictures more than the poems,' I said. 'There's something dreamlike about them, isn't there? Like you could step inside them and you might as well be in the stars.' I stopped, took a breath. 'I mean, they're beautiful, aren't they?' I blushed saying it, embarrassed, feeling stupid. But it was too late now to take it back. Sophie looked at me.

'I saw a drawing once of this boy climbing a ladder that was leaning against the moon. I think that was him,' she said. 'Anyway, that's what I'd like.'

'To draw?'

'To go to the moon.'

I laughed out loud, I couldn't help it. And now it was Sophie's turn to blush. 'No, that's good,' I said, still catching my breath and grinning. 'I've never been further than Halifax.'

That's when Sophie laughed, and that word came back into my head, like a beak jabbing me in my chest. Beautiful. I don't think I'd ever heard anything as beautiful as her laugh. Better than lark song, better than the call of the tawny owls at night. Beautiful.

'Have you ever seen a blackbird nest?' I asked.

We watched the nest as the sun rose, and watched the female guarding the eggs. Every now and then she'd get up as the male approached, and they'd have a sort of dance around the nest, getting in each other's way, and then she'd settle down again.

Once the sky was lit and the shadows were out, we walked back up to the paddock, and Sophie carried on towards the campervan, and with a wave of her hand that seemed suddenly very familiar to me, she said goodbye.

ELEVEN

I HAVE TO SAY something about Mam now, because there was a lot of rubbish talked about her in the papers and on TV when it all happened. And she was there before and she was there after, so it's right I should say what she wasn't. She wasn't some bad mam, and she wasn't a bad wife who didn't care what her husband got up to. She didn't let me run wild, not at all. She never wanted me to go live in the caravan, and she did all she could to stop me, apart from have me arrested. Or have John arrested. Because that's what it would have taken. And, no, I didn't run off to the caravan with John because Mam was rotten to me, or because we fell out. I'd rather have stayed, is the truth, right from the off. I'd much rather have slept in my comfy bed and got a proper tea, and soaked myself for an hour in a hot bath every other day. I'd rather have stayed in school, and I would have done if it wasn't for Otley. And if it hadn't been for John needing me, then I'd have stayed with Mam, too, and been safe and happy and I wouldn't have had to get up at the crack of dawn, and walk through woods and down lanes till my feet hurt, and I wouldn't have had to watch him die. But Ifs and Buts don't matter much in real life. John did need me, even if he'd never say. And that bastard Otley wasn't going to leave school or stop making my life hell, so it was down to me to go, wasn't it?

Mam knew it all, of course. And she knew why I went. And she tried to stop me, and she tried to save John. But some things can't be stopped, and this was one of them.

Mam says now that if you X-rayed my head, it would be full of birds' eggs and campion and blackberries in autumn. And she might be right. If you did the same to Sophie's, you'd just find a map of the stars. Mam's would be love, a headful of it. But John, if you'd X-rayed his head, I think it would have always been alive with beasts.

I don't mean monsters, but powerful and beautiful creatures. Things as random and elegant as the stars and the planets Sophie would talk about. He said everything we saw and everything we knew was made of the same startling stuff, and it was in us, in our blood, so if you thought about it, we contained the universe. Which was enough to make my head hurt, I can tell you. But what he meant, I think, was everything that was and everything that will be was coursing through our veins.

He told me about a deer in prehistoric Britain that stood taller than any deer alive, a head as large as an anvil with twelve-point antlers. He'd read it in a book. Like I said, John had read more books than anyone I knew. Sometimes at night, when he couldn't sleep, he'd get through three books, and by morning he'd have them packed in his bag for me to take back to the library.

He didn't care which books I brought back, as long as he could learn something from them. He didn't have any patience for made-up stories. He wanted facts, he said. 'I hear enough tall tales every day from folk for me to bother reading them.'

I'd get him books on war and kings and queens and times before when there were no cities and people had nothing but what they could carry. Because that's what I knew he liked most. Times when people would trek from place to place following the warm seasons, with nothing but a baby on their backs and what tools they'd crafted themselves.

John had learned how to make things from green wood, so you could shape it and bend it. Anything you can buy you can make, he said. He'd even got a stone bowl once and tried to smelt down a load of iron from the rocks in the quarry, but there wasn't enough heat. So when it didn't work he collected scrap metal from the local estates and melted down enough to make me a small knife, no bigger than a butter knife really, and he cast it with a thin handle, like how they did in the past. Then he wrapped cloth and leather around the handle for me to hold. I used to carry it around with me, because I loved it, that knife. But John told me it was only for the woods, and if anyone caught me with it in town I'd never hear the end of it, and neither would he.

Sometimes, he'd think so hard and he was so full of the words he'd read, that I could almost hear them hum in the quiet of the night when he struggled against sleep. I could tell when he was awake because the air seemed to be alive and he didn't have to make a noise or even move, but I knew he was lying with his eyes open, wishing it to be morning so he could put those words into practice.

'He has too many ideas,' Mam would say, back at the house, when we were together. 'It's not always wise to have so many.' A week after the party in the garden that never was, John had turned up, and it had taken him three days of sleeping in a bed before he'd camped in the backyard.

'He just needs to get it out of his system, that's all,' she'd said. And I remember once, after another row when John had stormed out, she'd looked at me and said, 'Be good when you're older, will you? Whatever you want to be, for God's sake, don't be an angry man.' Then straight after, nearly before she'd even finished, she'd apologised and told me to forget it, that he was good really, just his ideas were too much for her, too wayward and strong. John, she meant.

I'd given her a hug and she'd smiled and cried at the same time, like she did when things were bad. 'I'll never have ideas like him,' I'd told her. I was trying to make her stop crying, make her feel better, but I was telling the truth, too, because I wasn't like him, and I didn't have his mind.

'Good,' she'd told me, eyes shining like she was laughing. 'You'll be OK, then.' And she kissed my forehead.

I never knew what she meant, though, because ideas were good. Ideas were brave. It was ideas that put us on the moon and built undersea tunnels and stopped disease and infection and death. And for a bit I thought John was one of those men that would come up with an idea one day that would change everything. But time would prove me wrong and Mam right.

Anyway, this deer. I remember because usually when John read something he found rich and interesting, he'd talk about it for a day non-stop, but then you'd never hear about it again. Like he'd purged it. But this deer seemed to stick with him, and I got the sense it became fixed in his thoughts for weeks, coming back to him while we were out in the woods or washing in the stream. There we'd be, up to our ankles, and him slapping his clothes on a rock to dry and suddenly he'd straighten and look out to the trees, and he'd say something like, 'It was king of the tundra. When it was cold it thrived, and then woods came along and men and dogs, and the thing was just prey. Poor bugger,' he'd say, shaking his head, like he'd been talking about a friend he hadn't seen for a long time. Someone he'd heard had fallen on bad luck. Then he'd carry on what he was doing as though it had just been a fleeting idea and one he'd never voiced out loud. But for that moment, he was touched by the beggaring thing somehow. And I was, too.

It had bigger antlers than it needed, almost too big to carry, the stag.

'Like a crown,' John said. 'Like a great tree sprouting from its skull.' He seemed taken by that, but I couldn't see the point. Couldn't see why you'd have something that wasn't of use, that couldn't find you food or kill or dig. And in the end, it was the antlers that did for it. See, when men came along with the spring and the summer, they saw the deer was good for eating, and so they hunted it down, cornering it in amongst the close-set trees, where those antlers trapped it as good as spears stuck in the trunks.

And maybe that's what John saw in it. The tragedy, I mean. The vanity.

Because in the end, the one thing that made it glorious was the same thing that killed it.

TWELVE

THINGS WENT QUIET for a while after Toomey came that time. Every day I expected some other bugger to turn up and cause trouble with me, but they didn't, and things settled down and seemed to follow John's plan. I called him a couple of times, and I went over to Armley once more. The Leeds lawyer did what he'd promised, and checked in on me and asked if there was anything I needed, and I gave him the lunchbox, and he gave me some other cash, about two hundred quid, and neither of us talked about why. A lot of the stuff that went on was a mystery to me, and it wasn't until a long time later that I understood how it was connected. Not that it mattered by then, because John was dead, and nothing changes that. No matter how much you think and go over things in your mind, and no matter how much you pray things to change, they don't. What happens in the past stays done and dusted. John knew that better than anyone.

I saw Sophie again, but then it was time for her and her family to go. We said goodbye, and from the distance of the woods I watched the campervan pull away. I'd walk Mol in the fields after, and sometimes I'd stare over to the farm, as if by staring, the campervan would appear again, just like that. But it was gone, and for good.

It wasn't until just before John got out that I heard from her again.

It was Derby who gave me the card, and that wasn't all. When you think everything is running steady, that's when you should be on your guard, because you can bet something bad is just around the corner. And it was Derby who brought the bad with him.

'Fan mail for the wild boy of the woods,' he said, looking like he'd made the funniest joke in the world. Derby would take in any letters written to John, and every week or so we'd go up to the farmhouse and collect them. Derby himself didn't usually visit the caravan, but because I hadn't been for the post since John had got banged up, I suppose he thought he better come to me instead.

There were about four or five letters addressed to John, and one with my name on it.

'You got a sweetheart?' Derby said, waiting for me to open it, like he knew something that I didn't. I hate that, when people have one over you and they're perfectly happy letting you see it. 'Bit late for Valentine's day, isn't it?' It was a square blue envelope, and the writing with my name was small and neat. It wasn't Mam's writing, and I didn't know anyone else who'd bother writing to me, so I just held it and looked at it. Derby must have got bored waiting, because he harrumphed a bit, and made some other comments about the caravan, and didn't we ever clean up around here, and where did this dog come from, and will we be liable if it attacks anyone walking on the bridleways? It was cold that morning, with ice at the edges of the stream, and I could tell he wanted to see if I had a heater going in the van or something, so he could warm himself.

Me, I just nodded to Mol and said, 'She's too old to bite anything. She'd rather have a kip. Wouldn't you, girl?'

'Just make sure she's got a lead on while the sheep are in the fields. It's lambing time.'

I'd been washing the pan and the tea kettle and my mug in the stream when he'd arrived, and I'd just come out of the water, my arms still red with cold, when he climbed up into the van and wandered to the bedroom, poked open the door with a finger and looked inside.

'Nothing funny going on, is there?' he said, his breath clouding the air. 'Everything's all right, isn't it?'

I shoved the letters in my back pocket and followed him, pulled shut the bedroom door before he went inside. The rucksack with the gun was under the bed, but I'd hidden it well, so I wasn't worried he'd see it. I just didn't like him poking his nose in, that's all.

'John'll be back any day,' I said, hoping it would shut him up and get him on his way.

Derby was a chatty man, though. 'He could talk the hind legs off a donkey, that one,' was what John said. He wouldn't turn up much, but when he did he'd get his money's worth and go around the houses, talking this and that, stuff John didn't care about. I got the feeling he didn't have a lot of friends, and so he liked an hour or two chewing the fat with another man, someone he thought might share his worries about the council or the bank or his wife. So I was worried now that John wasn't here, he'd see me as a handy listener.

'Where is it you said he went again?' he asked.

'Nottingham,' I said, remembering what John had told me to say. 'He has a brother down there who's had an operation, so he's looking after him for a bit.' It was all a lie, of course. John didn't have a brother, and certainly not one in hospital. But Derby didn't know that.

'Nottingham?' Derby eyed me with his best poker face on, which was rubbish, if you ask me, and if he'd been a gambler he wouldn't have had a farm any more, or any clothes to stand up in for that matter.

'That's right,' I said, trying to sound sure.

John, on the other hand, had the best poker face you'd ever see. You never knew if what he said was true or not. I hadn't seen anyone lie like John. Not that he lied all the time, and not big ones. But the way things were you had to tell the odd fib or two to keep going, he knew that. Well, when he was in the mood he could tell a right whopper and keep a straight face, and even I'd believe him. But I wasn't like that. I was no better than Derby. No, I was a bad liar at the best of times, so it took a real effort to look hard-faced when I was talking nonsense. 'He's back soon. Maybe even tomorrow. Is there anything you want me to ask him?'

'Matter of fact, there is. You both know this arrangement only works if you two keep out of trouble. It's not exactly legal what John and you are up to, living here. You do know that?'

I didn't know it, not really. I mean, I knew not many other people lived like this, and I knew I had to make sure the schools didn't see me tramping through the woods in case they asked me what I was up to. Although if they did, John told me to say I was being home-schooled, and there was nothing they could do about it.

We always looked out for the coppers, too, of course.

'Well, the thing is, you haven't kept out of trouble, have you?' Derby said. 'I needed John to keep his nose clean, and he didn't, did he?'

'He did,' I said, struggling to steady my voice.

'Don't try it on with me,' Derby said, pretending to be tough, which he wasn't. Not at all. He was yellow enough, because I'd seen him in rows with John, and he always backed down, every time. But today it looked like Derby had found a spine, because he was dead confident when he said, 'Unless this brother of his is convalescing in Armley Gaol then what you just told me is a load of whitewash, lad. You think I was born yesterday? The silly sod's got himself nicked, hasn't he? I know, so don't bother covering up for him.'

'He's in Nottingham,' I said. 'He'll be back soon and you can ask him yourself.'

'This isn't up for discussion.' He rummaged for something in the pocket of his coat. 'I haven't come to negotiate with you or your father. Here, this is a letter from my solicitor for you to vacate my land, and if you don't, then I'll call in the police and you'll be helping your dad look after that dying brother of his in prison.'

I grabbed the letter and looked at it, but my mind was too busy for me to take in any of the writing. 'But you can't. We live here,' I said, adding, 'He'll be back this week,' which was the bit that wasn't a lie.

He must have taken the letter back, or maybe I gave it to him, because next thing he slapped it down on the table, hard, and turned for the door. 'I'm not an uncharitable man,' he said, looking sort of embarrassed. 'I know this isn't your doing, so you can wait until your father gets back. But then you need to get your things out of here, all right? After that, you're on your own and I won't be held responsible for what the coppers do to you.'

When he was gone I shoved the letter in a drawer, and sat in the bedroom and held Mol and I cried. I'm not proud of it, but I didn't know what else to do, because everything looked bad then. I was sick of being alone, sick of being cold, sick of living in the muck. Right then I could have happily burned the caravan down and just set off walking, and not worried where I ended up or if I ever saw John again, or guns or cash or anything.

Then I remembered the envelope with my name. It was late when I opened it, and I looked at it by the light of the paraffin lamp.

It turned out to be a card not a letter.

The picture on the front was a painting of the moon, with this smiling blue bird flying across it. Not a real bird, like a jay or a blue tit, but what John would call a picture-book bird, which meant it was no bird that ever existed. My eyes were raw and my nose was still running, and I couldn't read it too well. I think I went over it two or three times before I took it in, even though it was only a few lines.

Mr Derby told me he'd pass on a card, so I thought I'd write and say hi. I didn't tell you, but it was my birthday this week, and I got a new phone. Here's the number, just in case you want to say hi. And our new address. If you want to meet up some time, text.

PS: I hope the blackbird chicks are thriving. x

It was signed *Sophie*, and there was a mobile number written at the bottom of the card in small, very neat letters. I folded it up and shoved it in the pocket of my coat, and that night I wandered into the fields while Mol sniffed after rabbits, and I stared into the dark, hoping I might see a little light blink on somewhere, one that was just for me and no one else. Not Jupiter or the North Star, just a light on a campervan.

But the dark was just dark, and after an hour or so I went back and I fell asleep and I didn't have any dreams that night, which I was happy about.

The next day, John came home. Without me knowing it, those wolves that were asleep underground were waking up, and soon they'd be clawing their way out into the sunlight. And it was too late to stop them now.

PART TWO

THIRTEEN

'WE'LL HAVE TO keep our heads down for a few days, at least,' John said. 'Everything nice and quiet, and no bother.'

He was unpacking a black bin bag he'd brought home from Armley, taking out some unwashed clothes. The gun was still in the rucksack on the floor of the bedroom. It had been the first thing he'd seen to when he got back, before even having a cup of tea or getting some kip. He took out the gun, pulled away the rubber band and the plastic bag around the trigger and stock. Then he set about rubbing the thing all over with a cloth.

'You're never to touch this, got it?' he said, without looking at me. He was on his knees, cleaning the gun. 'But if you ever do, if you ever have to, you're never to touch it with your bare hands, understand? Gloves at all times.' I'd noticed that he hadn't taken off the gloves he'd been wearing when he arrived. I'd just thought he might be cold, because the last days had been freezing. 'Same goes for the shells. Did you touch these?'

There'd been another plastic bag, a small white one, and I hadn't bothered opening it, but you could tell by how heavy it was that there was a box in there, with things rattling inside it.

'No, just the gun,' I said. 'Is it yours?'

'I'll just be borrowing it for a bit.' He tore open the white bag, and took out this big square box that said *12 gauge* on it. He didn't open the box, just shoved it into a large black felt bag he'd brought with him, with a string tie at the top. After he'd finished with the gun, he wrapped it in the oily rag and put that in the felt bag, too. Then he took the whole lot and put it in the steel tool box and locked it, and shoved it back in its place under the van. 'He didn't see the box, yeah?' he said, when he came back inside.

'Who?'

'Toomey, when he came. The man in the Range Rover. Did he see you under the van?'

'No,' I said. Then, 'Is he a mate?'

'He's given me work in the past, that's all. He's got money and connections, sorted me out with legal advice.'

'Do you like him?'

'Not really. Do you?'

I shook my head. 'He said you might teach me how you work.'

'Did he?' John looked up at me. 'Well, he was wrong. I'm never going to teach you anything about how I get money. Did he touch anything else in here?'

'Don't think so.'

'Well, did he or not?'

Since John had got back, he'd hardly asked anything about how I'd been doing or how I was. It was all business, like he was ticking off some list in his head, and I didn't matter. I wondered if this is what prison does to you, makes you mechanical, like a robot. I was thinking about those boxes people like to put you in.

'I asked you a question.'

I tried to remember when Toomey had come, what we'd said and where he'd been.

'He sat at the table and stroked Mol for a bit,' I said. 'Then he went out. That's all. And he unlocked the padlock on the door somehow.' John was standing with his hands on his hips, looking around the place, nodding. 'Can I keep her?' I asked, after a bit.

John stared at me like he didn't know what I was on about, but he did. I'd seen it as soon as he'd set eyes on her. He'd been working out if she was a nuisance or not, how much she'd cost to keep. I'd been holding my breath all this time, right from the moment I'd seen him tramping down from the field. 'I like her,' I said. 'She's nice, and I want to keep her.'

Mol was lying on her side at the end of the caravan, her belly rising and falling as she slept.

'Well, can I?'

'She can eat leftovers, and if she causes any trouble, she'll have to go,' he said.

'She'll behave,' I said, grinning. 'Thanks, John.'

'Hang on. Come here,' he said.

He was looking dead serious, so I didn't know whether he was going to tell me off about something or not. I tried to work out in my head what I might have done wrong. I looked around the van to see if there was anything I'd forgotten, then I stepped slowly over to John, and for a moment I thought he was going to clout me. But he just held me by the arms above my elbows and stared into my face.

'You know I love you, don't you,' he said. 'You're the only person that I do love, I need you to know that. You do, don't you?' he said.

His cheeks were trembling when he said it. His beard had started to grow back, and he'd put a bit of weight on inside. The way he was looking at me made me feel like I might cry, because *he* looked like he might cry, and I'd never seen him like that before. Only the rages and the fits, but not this. This was different. It frightened me.

'Yeah,' I said. My mouth wouldn't work, so I had to say it again, louder, 'Yeah, course I do.'

He was strong, and he was holding me hard, hurting me. But it wasn't on purpose, I knew that.

'Things will be different,' he said, and he pulled me against his chest and started hugging me. 'I promise you,' he said. 'Soon, you'll see.' And I hugged him back, and now I was proper crying, and I didn't want him to see me cry, so I buried my face in his coat and held it there until the tears stopped.

We must have been like that for five minutes, both of us shaking, and afterwards we didn't mention what had happened or what we'd said. We just got on with things, and it was only when I was falling asleep that night that I realised that I hadn't mentioned what Derby had said about us having to go. I thought about waking John up and saying something – looking back, that's exactly what I should have done, of course – but he was already snoring out loud, and so tomorrow would have to do, I thought, and I leaned in closer to Mol, who was on the fold-out cot with me. And soon enough I was asleep, too.

FOURTEEN

WHEN THE WORLD ends things get simpler than you imagine.

It's not like the films. You don't need a gun or a hammer or a bomb, and you don't need maps, because where are you going to go when the land is laid to waste? You don't need petrol or a car or a crossbow either.

'Those things are for comic books,' John would say, without looking up from whatever he was doing, cutting twine or plucking a pigeon or lighting a handful of tinder. He was always busy with something while the sun was up. It was a thing with him not to be lazy, not to waste time because to him doing nothing was like waiting for death.

'No,' he'd tell me, concentrating so hard his eyes would shine like pewter, 'what you need are three things. Just three. And those three things are all free and here and there's no shortage of them. And that's why people are the stupidest species on this earth and why they're all going to hell.'

Shelter, Food and Water.

That'll see you right when it all breaks down.

I never knew what he meant when he talked like that, because he wasn't an end-of-the-world nutter, no matter what they said in the papers afterwards. He was the opposite. He thought the world would

never end, because no matter what we did to it, it would just go on.

'It's bigger than us,' he'd say, 'and if time is an hour we're just on Earth for less than a fraction of a second.'

No, it was people he had a problem with, not the Earth, and mostly people who told other people what to do all the time. He hated Big Heads and Braggers and Bullies.

'Like Otley at school,' I'd say. 'Otley's a bully.'

'Yeah, him and others. But the thing is, we can stop them by not fearing them.'

I didn't get what he meant.

'Well, see, people like Otley and the others, they can't exist without us, but we can exist without them. You can bet Otley comes to school every day hoping you'll be there. So he can have his fun with you. But you don't, do you?'

'No, I wish he never came to school.'

'Well then, he can't do without you. He needs you.'

I still didn't get it.

'Remember ticks, yeah?' Another thing John was big on was ticks. Which is why we had to check ourselves when we'd been in the woods, and after Mol came along I'd spend all evening looking over her belly and legs for them. Because if you got one of those bloodsuckers on you, you'd know about it. And it might make you ill for the rest of your life, John said. Because they had poison in them.

I hated the horrible things, especially when they swelled fat and purple, like blood blisters.

'Ticks are parasites,' I'd say.

John shook his head. 'There are no parasites in nature. You think about that. Everything brings something to another creature or habitat. Rats, fleas, worms, they all contribute, all have a purpose, even if it's just to control a population. Plants, too. Ivy and toothwort and dodder. Yellow rattle doesn't kill the grass, but it holds it back and lets other flowers and plants gain a foothold. You get a flea, and it can pass on immunities from one creature to another. No, the only parasites in the world are men, you remember that. Nothing else feeds off something else so hungrily, nothing kills it so quickly and ruthlessly.'

He hadn't been talking about Otley any more, and he hadn't been talking about ticks. He'd been talking about Toomey. Not that he'd said it out loud, but now I know. And I think about that postcard he liked, *The Flea*. Because that's not its name.

I remember now, it's called *The Ghost of a Flea*. John had told me.

He'd said, 'Back in the past, people thought the souls of bad people got stuck in a flea, and that's what Blake saw when he painted that picture. He saw a ghost appear before him. Not the flea itself, but its soul.'

Now that it's all over, when I think of Toomey I don't see the smug bloke sat in my caravan in his black suit. I see the bloodsucker on the postcard, with a threat of Pain and Blood and Death. And maybe on that night, looking back, I think John did, too.

FIFTEEN

THE NEXT DAY was Saturday, and my eyes were stuck together when I woke, and my head ached a bit. It was dark, and the caravan smelled of old socks and mud and sweat, and so did I. The last week had been cold enough for the stream to freeze, and I hadn't had the courage to have a proper wash for about four days now.

There was a noise in the van, and I looked to see John packing his rucksack on the kitchen top.

'Are you off somewhere?' I'd slept on the cot, and in the night Mol had left me to go with John on the bed. I didn't know where I was straight away. I was still trying to open my eyes. 'John, what's up?'

'We're both going away for a bit. I'm packing some of your things. Just a couple of nights, somewhere fancy. Hot showers, as much as you like.'

'Real life?'

'Real life,' John said, a smirk in his voice in the dark, like the cat that got the cream.

'But didn't you say to keep our heads down?'

'That's exactly what we'll be doing.'

'What is it? Where we off?'

'You'll see. Bring whatever else you think you'll need, but no more, because we'll be walking.'

'Can Mol come?'

He looked to the dog laid out on the floor of the bedroom. 'Yeah, we'll take her. Be a holiday for her, too, eh?'

It had tried to snow, and the weeds and undergrowth were topped with frost and ice. It creaked underfoot while we walked.

'What about the seedlings?'

John had planned this week to seed all the veg for summer, put them in pots behind the screens. Beans and marrow and potatoes.

'Better wait till the weather picks up.' He was striding on ahead, moving through the trees with his head held high, like he was sniffing the air. A halo of heat around him, bright as the moonlight. He was carrying the big bag, his army issue, and the tent and bedrolls, and he was wearing so many layers that he looked like a giant loping between the trees, like nothing could stop him. If one of those bison from the European forest had reared up in front of us I was sure John would have walked right over it without blinking or even getting out of breath.

Times like this he looked indestructible, some warrior from one of his books, half forest, half man. He might have been a hunter back in the days of stag and bear, lost in the cage of trees but free, too, living as wild as them. Times like these, I'd forget the nights when he'd been cowering in Mam's backyard, and sobbing, like it was another man. And that was our mistake, because he was all of it at once – warrior and soldier and crying lad. And criminal.

'Catch this,' he said, throwing the bag with the tent rods and camping stove at me. I slung it across my shoulder, glad of the weight, because I was like him, then. And for a moment I saw us from a distance, like strangers – just two blokes in loads of gear, marching through the trees. And in my head it could have been any time, any century, and we could have been any two blokes who had ever lived.

In the half light of morning, we stopped to watch two hares in a stand-off on the horizon, their ears and backs all slender and slick as rusty water, ready to box. John got a cheese sandwich out of his bag and tore it in half, gave one half to me. The air was blue and pretty. We both loved mornings like these, when the sky was still clap-cold, and the stiff, upturned soil of the fields appeared to sparkle.

'What was nick like?' I asked, biting into the sandwich. Nick was prison, was gaol, was bang-up.

'Nick's just like school, but there's no lessons. So you just sit about getting on each other's nerves. But I'm used to it, because of the army. Others aren't, so they get all riled up and want to get in a fight.'

'Did you have to fight anyone?'

John smiled. 'If you know how to fight you never need to fight,' he said. It was another one of those things he'd say that I never understood, because at school the kids who were good at fighting did it all the time. You couldn't stop them. I'd seen lads getting into fights about nothing, and seen kids losing teeth and smiling about it. So don't tell me if you're hard you never have to prove it.

I wondered what Sophie would make of this – me in the middle of nowhere, with John, watching hares as the sun came up. It was things like this I missed telling her, now she was gone. Not that I ever told her much about John in the first place, but something in the way she looked at me gave me the idea she knew more than she let on. Had she guessed John had been banged up all that time?

The sandwich tasted good, but part of me wished I was back in Mam's house, asleep and happy and not even thinking what was out in the world, waiting for me. Not thinking about those ancient beasts under the soil, wanting out. And it made me feel guilty, like I was betraying him by even thinking about being happier. That's how I felt every time I mentioned Mam – like it was against the rules.

My thoughts must have been easy to see again, like they were written on my forehead, because John asked, 'You miss her, don't you?'

'Course I do,' I said.

'Didn't you see her when I was inside?'

I didn't answer straight away, because I didn't know how he'd take it.

'Once, yeah.'

John just ate his half and sipped the tea from his flask, before handing the flask to me.

'She all right?' he asked, like he didn't mind me talking about her if I wanted to. But his voice was flat, and there was something in his eyes that made me wary.

'She said she'd like me home more.'

The hares ran off after sparring for a bit,
then me and John and Mol walked on, and by
the time the sun was high in the sky we'd
crossed the A road and gone down into the valley,
over a river and through fields ploughed with rape, the
low green stalks already higher than my knees. We walked four
hours or more, and as we walked we scared quail up out of the grass,
and partridge, and rabbits. There was a deer or two, too, but only in
the distance. We passed a farm with a wire fence where some bastard
had hung twelve dead moles. We crossed an empty stream. We saw a
burned-out car rusting in a field.

We'd not gone this far before and I started to worry whether
I could go much further without a rest when we turned down
into a village and John said we could stop at the pub and have
a sit down, if I liked.

'Wait here, all right?' John dropped his gear on a timber bench
in the beer garden at the back. 'You need the bog?'
Bog was the toilet, the gents, the crapper. I
shook my head. 'I'll be out in a while, don't
leave the stuff, yeah? Get the dog some water.'

He went inside, and I didn't think anything of it, because why
would I? Everything seemed sort of simple that morning, with John.

Which is how he wanted it. I didn't even notice the name of the place, and it wasn't until the police told me later that I learned what it was called, and where we'd been. How far it was.

It's sort of impressive how much John had in his head, all these different things going on, and all of it hidden. Most of it, anyway. And part of me hates him for it, and always will. The lies, I mean. Because he always made me feel like crap when I lied, or even when I didn't lie but didn't tell him everything. Like Mam, like going to see her, which I'd told him about in the end. But the look on his face was like I'd done something wrong by not telling him sooner. And there he was, lying his face off, and not even feeling bad about it. And that pub wasn't even the start.

SIXTEEN

I<small>T'S TRUE WHAT</small> I'd told him, by the way, about Mam.

I'd gone over to see her in the third week John was banged up. I hadn't meant to, not really.

I had but I hadn't.

I'd gone to town with those library books I'd got out in Leeds, because I'd forgotten that I'd have to renew them or else I'd get a fine, and we couldn't afford fines. I'd mooched about the library a bit, getting warm, and looking at books about ancient Britain. I thought I might see pictures of those buffalo and bison that John had seen, but all there was were pictures of a stag that the book said would be as tall as a bus, maybe. Finally, I went to the poetry section and found William Blake and started looking through those poems John used to read out loud.

The book was called *Songs of Innocence and of Experience*.

I pored over them, taking them all in. But when I read them, somehow the words stayed stuck on the page. I couldn't make them sound like John made them sound, couldn't make them ring loud like he did, even when I spoke them out to myself. When John read them they seemed full of the world and its colours, like he'd written them himself. Like the words were birds and while they were printed in the book those birds were stuck, caged. It was only when he read them that they flew. And I couldn't do it, didn't have the knack, and maybe I'd never learn. That's what I thought, and maybe it's true, but even now I still try to get them up and going when the feeling takes me.

After the library, I wandered up to the estate. I knew she might be there, because Wednesdays, she worked the dayshift at the nursing home, Fridays, too. Today was a Tuesday, which was a night shift, so of course she might be at her house, might see me from her window. I was hoping for it maybe, but quietly.

Before the war, before all of it began, before I was here, Mam had lived on the Walker estate and worked behind the bar in the social club. That's where she met John, because him and the others from the barracks would go in there when they had leave and Get Drunk and Cause Havoc.

I passed the club. It had closed down ages ago, and its windows were boarded up now, the tattered Union flag still flapping against the chimney. Mol stopped in the empty car park and squatted down to pee. It took a while, and I saw that maybe her hips were getting stiffer. Maybe she was ten or twelve, or however old old dogs are.

'Who's your friend?'

Mam smiled over at me, her arms folded against the wind. She was on the pavement, looking tired and pretty and everything I'd missed. When I didn't say anything, she cocked her head to one side, and half-turned to the road. 'I'm off to the shops. Want to walk with me?' And she knew I did.

We'd looked around the shops, gone up to the park with Mol and let her run for a bit. Then when we were coming back, me carrying a bag of shopping and Mam carrying another, Mam had asked about John. 'So how long is he in for this time?'

'How d'you know?'

'I'm not daft, no matter what you think. It's a small town, and word gets around.'

I wanted to say I never thought she was daft, not once. She was the only one in the world I thought had her head on right, is the truth. So I told her what had happened, and why, with John and the coppers and the big houses, but not Toomey or the gun or anything stupid that would just make her worry.

'He says it'll be another week at most. Not long.'

'Too long for you to be out in the caravan on your own,' she said. 'Why don't you come home? You're not doing him any good by getting pneumonia.'

'I'm fine. I've got to look after the garden.'

'You mean the veg? Isn't it too early for planting?'

'Some of it, yeah. But the leeks are already up.'

The road was quiet and the wind had died down. Mol was walking ahead of us, looking back every now and then to see we were still there. Nervous and happy at the same time, and eager for the attention of a stranger.

'You didn't come to court,' I said then. 'I bet he'd have liked to have seen you.'

'Good job for you I didn't, because no way I'd have put up with you staying in that van on your own all this time.'

'Yeah but—'

'And no, he wouldn't have liked to have seen me,' Mam said, interrupting. She didn't sound sad or annoyed or anything really. She just sounded like Mam. 'He'd have been angry, and we both know it. He'd have looked daggers at me and he'd have not talked to you for weeks after.' She stopped and looked me in the face, kindly and calm. 'You can come home with me now. You can have a bath and something to eat. Stay the night, at least.'

'Can't,' I said, which was a lie. Because I could have done and John wouldn't have known. But there was this feeling I was doing something wrong just by being there, letting him down somehow.

'Your dog could do with a bath,' Mam said, nodding down to Mol.

I didn't even know you were supposed to bath dogs, but I'd noticed her fur smelled a bit, and her paws were grubby. Her yellow coat was sort of brown now on her belly and on her legs.

'A bath, maybe, yeah,' I said, after a while. 'OK. But don't tell him.'

'Are you sure someone's not looking for her? Maybe we should tell the RSPCA? What does it say on her tag? Is there a phone number?'

I didn't want to talk about Mol or where she came from. I didn't want to talk about any of that. I wanted Mam and me and John to be together, to forget about the van and the woods, and Toomey.

'When he comes out we're going to move to Scotland,' I said, suddenly. 'You can come, too, he wants you to.'

'That's nice. But you know I've got a life here.'

'He says they need people, Mam. There's this place where they need teachers and nurses and people to look after sheep and chickens, and we could live there and grow our own food. All of us together.' Which was all true, I wasn't lying. John had shown me the articles in the newspaper about whole islands that needed people to come and live and work.

Mam just stared at me and didn't say anything else until we got to her house. She heated up some soup while I watched TV, and then she went upstairs and ran a bath.

'Is he still taking his medication?' she asked, once we'd got Mol in the water and were rubbing her coat with soap.

'Sometimes.'

'You see him take the pills?'

I had to think about it. 'Before he was banged up, yeah,' I said.

'Every day?'

I was grinning because Mol looked all skinny when she was wet. Skinny and a bit sad, but in a funny way, like she was putting it on for us. And I had to laugh when she looked at me with those grey glassy eyes as I rinsed off her back.

'I said, have you seen him take his medication every day?' Mam repeated. 'You know he needs proper help, don't you? You can't look after him. I couldn't, so you can't.' She put down the soap, looked at her wet hands in her lap. 'What do you think he'll do when he gets some money?' she asked.

'I think he'll do what he says, and settle down, grow vegetables and work on farms.'

'You think that'll make him happy?'

'He says it will.'

'And you believe him.'

I looked up at her and saw the late sun flash in the mirror behind her head, and I shut one eye against it, and said, 'Don't you?'

'I think your father and happiness don't have the easiest of relationships. I think they barely know each other. I think he has a fire in him that won't stop at simple happiness, because that's what happened before, and we don't change over time, we just get more like ourselves. Him more than most.'

Mam wasn't one for making speeches, and that was probably the most she'd said in months that wasn't to tell me to look after myself and she loved me. It was something she'd been thinking about for a long time, I guessed, even if she didn't know herself she'd been thinking it. I understood most of it, but not all, and her and him were the same in that way.

'Couldn't you make him happy?' I said. 'If we went to Scotland, if we lived together?'

'He'd grow tired of that sort of happiness in a while, and then where would he go? He'd be stuck on an island with you and me and a load of sheep. He'd hate it.'

'But it's what he wants.'

'Men like John have to be saved from what they want sometimes,' she said.

I must have looked at her like I didn't understand, which I didn't. There was a hardness in her voice I hadn't heard before.

'If we did that, we'd be trapping him, and he'd not just hate the life, but us, too. Don't you see that?'

I didn't see that, but I didn't say so. I just stared up at her face, splashed as it was by sun and by a fever of light that made her cheeks blush.

'Maybe I can make him happy,' I said, feeling annoyed suddenly, because why couldn't I help? Just because Mam couldn't in the past, didn't mean I couldn't now. Things change, I wanted to say. And maybe I could be the one that changes it all, makes him better, stops him from getting worse. Why not me? It was me that calmed him when he was raging, after all. Me that got him to sleep when all he wanted to do was kick and punch. Me that was looking after him in the woods.

I wanted to say all this, but I kept my mouth shut and smiled at Mol and scrubbed her belly with my fingers and got her to let out a happy whimper.

'You're not in danger, are you?' Mam said then. 'If you are, you know what you need to do, right?'

'I know,' I said.

She'd told me plenty of times, long before I went to live with him. I had to call the police, then call her. Make sure I was away from him, somewhere safe. Not because he'd want to hurt me, he wouldn't. He'd never. But maybe he'd hurt me by accident or maybe he just wanted to hurt himself, and I'd get in the way.

'I'm not in danger,' I said. 'He's OK. Anyway, he's in nick, so he can't hurt anyone, can he?'

'And what happens when he gets out?'

Mam looked at me with this look that I couldn't work out. So much going on in it, I felt lost. The sleeves of her jumper were wet and when she wiped her cheek it made her face wet, and the loose strands of her hair were wet, too. She looked angry and upset and loving and worried.

'Well, he's got the Job,' I said, before I could stop myself.

'What job?'

I'd been showing off, trying to prove her wrong, being a Big Head. John had warned me about that before, plenty of times. 'Don't show off, and don't be a Big Head. It'll come back and bite you on your arse,' he'd say. 'Always does, every time.'

'Has someone given him a job?' Mam asked. She picked up a towel and was drying her hands.

I'd already said too much, but if I just kept quiet she'd know. So I said, 'Not a *job* job. But there's work, he says. Something on the horizon.'

She looked at me funny, because I never said 'something on the horizon', and I don't know why it came to me then. Don't know where I'd heard it.

'. . . And if he saves up, we'll try to get that croft,' I added, quickly, hoping she wouldn't notice. 'And we'll get goats because they're tougher than sheep. And Mol will like it.'

Mam said nothing, but she sensed something because she didn't mention John's name again that evening. While she cooked tea, I had a soak myself, the first bath I'd had since summer last, which felt odd and too hot and too wet, because I'd got used to splashing in the stream every day. And after we'd eaten, I went around my bedroom, picking up this and that, old toys and stuff. Mam had kept it all as I'd left it, but it seemed changed somehow. Familiar in a way, but more like a memory of someone else's life, not mine. It was nice, though, sleeping in my own bed, and in the morning when Mam woke me, for a moment, I'd forgotten I'd ever lived in the van in the woods. Forgotten all about the beasts in the ground and the smell of moss and cold and dirt. Forgotten the secrets me and John shared, forgotten the lies.

'Everything's all right, isn't it, darling?' she asked, while she boiled some eggs for breakfast. The kitchen was filled with sun, and Mam's face looked real young right then, younger than I ever remembered. 'You two – you'll be all right, won't you?'

She had this proper worried expression on her face when she said it, so I nodded and smiled, and told her, 'Yeah, course. We'll be fine.'

But when I left she just gave me a kiss and said 'Take care', and didn't hug me like she usually did. And I knew she'd heard the lie in my voice.

SEVENTEEN

I WAS STILL SITTING outside the pub, in the cold, when Benny showed up.

He'd been inside all along, of course, with John. They'd arranged it, but I didn't know. I didn't know much back then. I didn't know why we'd bothered to trek four hours in the cold, or what John had been doing in the pub for thirty minutes while I froze my arse off outside.

'All right, kidda?' Benny said, without looking at me. He was standing by the wall, shielding a match from the wind as he tried to light his fag. He always called me kidda. I'd got used to being called different things by different blokes, and all of them without fail thought they were being funny. Kidda, squire, squirt, fella, me lad. One of the blokes, this sarky bloke with a racing green Jag who'd come see John on Sundays used to call me Chilblain. And every time he laughed like it was the funniest thing he'd ever heard.

'Morning, Chilblain,' he'd say. 'See you later, Chilblain.' Laughing all the time, like he was some genius who'd come up with a joke that struck comedy gold, and I was the lucky one he was sharing it with.

Benny, though, he called me kidda. Which I didn't mind, because he didn't make me feel like the joke was on me. He was all right, was Benny, compared to the others.

'Nice dog,' he said, sucking on the cigarette. 'Retriever mix, isn't she?'

'Thanks,' I said, trying not to look surprised that he was here, outside this particular pub in the middle of nowhere on the very same day me and John had arrived. 'You all right?' I asked.

'Not bad,' he said. 'Busy, which is just how I like it. He'll be out soon,' he added, meaning John. And I nodded, like I already knew but thanks anyway.

When Benny had finished his fag, he went back inside and I got up and dragged Mol around the beer garden for a bit, trying to warm us both up. I was so angry that I could have happily walked back home right then, if I'd known the way. I thought about it, too. With a bit of luck, I could have retraced our steps and got us back without too much bother. But if I did just go I wouldn't get the chance to tell him how pissed off I was, would I? And I wanted him to know. Because I hated being left in the dark. Hated being treated like a kid. And by *him* of all people, who always told me to never let people talk down to me or patronise me, and never take any whitewash.

It was another ten minutes before he came out, him and Benny together. They shook hands and John handed over a wad of cash to Benny, then Benny got in a white van and went off.

I waited until the van was out of sight and then I said, 'What's all this about? How come you didn't tell me?'

John was surly and quiet and he didn't look at me. He picked up his gear and threw it over his shoulder.

'Hey, I'm talking,' I said.

'It's business,' he said. 'Nothing to do with you.'

'Then why the bloody hell am I here?'

'We're on holiday. I told you. So pack in the interrogation.'

He was in a mood all right, I could see it in his face. One of his odd moods where you didn't know if he'd start shouting at you or hugging you. I guessed he'd had a pint, too. Maybe more than one. Which always made things harder with him.

'You just said it was business, John. Just now, you said it. You'd planned to meet Benny here, so why didn't you just tell me?'

He went quiet again, but he didn't start walking. He just stood there, breathing heavy, like he'd been running and he had to catch some air.

'What did you buy off him?'

'He's getting a bike for me, that's all. A motorbike.'

'Is it for the Job?'

John nodded.

'Are you going to tell me what it is? Well, are you? John?'

'It's a robbery.'

'A house?' I said, and my face was hurting now, like I wanted to cry but I couldn't. I wasn't going to, not in front of him. 'One of those big houses?'

'No, not one of those. It's a different job.'

An old couple came walking out of the pub, looking at us and at each other, then at us again, as they walked to their car. They shook their heads as they climbed in, like they couldn't believe what they were seeing. Like we were an embarrassment or something. I wanted to tell them to mind their own business, and sling their hook. But John had his head down, not moving, silent, waiting for them to go. So I did the same. The engine of the car started up, and the woman, she stared at her stuck-up husband and he mouthed something back to her, and then they set off down the road.

'Were you ever going to tell me?' I said. I was almost yelling now, and my hands were shaking. Mol gave off a little bark, and I leaned down and stroked her neck, trying to calm her. 'Were you?'

'Course I was,' John said. His face was blank, and his voice was so low and steady it got me worried. It was when he was calm things went wrong sometimes, when he'd suddenly go off on one. I'd seen it before, so I sort of held my breath and hoped this time wouldn't be like that. 'I'm telling you now, aren't I?' he said, sounding all reasonable, like teachers at school. Like I was thick and they had to talk really slow so I'd get the message. 'It's a big job, and I'll need you to help me. That's the truth. So you're going to have to pull yourself together or you'll be no use to anyone.' He lifted a hand out to me, palm up, as though to calm me. 'Well, can you do that? Can you pull it together?'

I wasn't done yet. I still had a lot to say, and a lot I wanted to tell him. Like how he always went on about how people fool themselves and pretend to be something they're not. Like it was the Real Way of Seeing the World and he had the knack and everyone else was a Faker. But the thing was, he was the same as them. He'd say one thing and do another, like there were different rules for him. Like with the thing about robbing houses, or what he said about reading books and blokes ending up in gaol. Or how it was all right for him to get banged up, but not for me. Not that I had any plan to go to gaol, or the army. You couldn't drag me into them. But that wasn't the point.

I bit my lip and held myself in the cold until I stopped shaking.

And after a while John nodded and waved his hand to follow him.

We walked down the road a couple of miles to a bus stop. And we waited in silence until a bus arrived, and we got on and John paid our fare, and the bus took us across the moors and out to the coast, and by the time it was getting dark we were sitting on the beach, listening to the sea on the shore.

'Don't you tell anyone,' John said, his voice low and quiet in the night. 'If you do, Toomey'll kill me. It's between you and me, all right?'

'All right,' I said.

And then John told me the plan.

EIGHTEEN

THERE WAS THIS betting shop. Actually, there was more than one, but the one John was interested in was on the high street in Sedworth, and that was the Job. It was owned by a bloke named Hazlit, and Hazlit and Toomey didn't get on because they both had betting firms and Toomey wanted to show Hazlit who was boss. And Hazlit's business wasn't run the best, and so he had money onsite. So every couple of days, when the betting shops totted up what they'd taken in cash, the blue security van would come and pick it up and take it to the bank. But Hazlit's security was cheap, and the men who ran it were old, and so Toomey wanted them robbed. Just once. He wasn't interested in the money, John said, so John could keep what he nicked. And sometimes these vans carried up to a million quid, he said. But not this one, because Toomey wasn't so stupid as to let us have a fortune. What he was interested in was sending a message to Hazlit – that he shouldn't step on people's toes, that he shouldn't get too big for his breeches, that he should show respect and stay within his own boundaries, and there was enough money for all of them if they played it smart and didn't get greedy.

Just a robbery with no violence, a wave of the shotgun, should be enough to scare off the old geezers. And that was that, no harm done.

It sounded simple. If John did it right, Hazlit wouldn't even call the police, he said, because he'd know it was Toomey sending a message. He'd done it before with other fellas. A phone call would be made or something would be dropped in the post, letting them know it was purely business between the two firms. So there was no risk, as long as everything went as planned.

To me, though, the whole thing sounded risky. John telling me to keep my lips buttoned or Toomey would kill him sounded like one big, terrible risk. You couldn't get any bigger, was what I was thinking. But did I say anything? Too right, I didn't, I just sat and nodded, like what he told me made complete sense.

When he'd done with the story, and we were looking out to the sea, out to the black where the gulls slept afloat, I realised I'd been thinking about what Mam said, and I tried to imagine what it was like for them before I arrived. And I said, 'Do you believe in luck, John?'

He turned to me in the dark. 'Luck's just another word for accidents, and there's plenty of them about. According to my mam, I was an accident. So yes, I believe in luck.'

'Do you believe in God?' I asked him.

'I never really had time to think about it. But the men I knew who did, some of them were killed anyway, and so it didn't seem to help them much. Do *you* believe in God?'

'I pray sometimes, so maybe I do.' The truth was I'd prayed plenty, of course, but I didn't know who to, exactly. Just words at night, before sleep.

'What do you pray for?'

'For you,' I said.

John didn't say anything for a while. 'Well, with my luck and your prayers, maybe we'll be OK then, eh?' he said, at last.

We'd pitched the tent in a field at the top of the cliff that looked over a little town with a single steep lane that led from the flat, wide rocks of the coast, up past shops selling fossils and black jet and fishing nets and sweets and postcards, to a couple of campsites. At the site, there was a shower block with boiling hot water, and even a little sheltered patio where you could sit under the outdoor heaters that were fixed to the edge of the red-tiled roof and glowed pink like fire. Maybe it wasn't as fancy as John had made out, but you don't know what it's like to have the luxury of hot water on tap and heaters when you've lived in a sardine can for half a year. Mol loved the heaters, and no matter how hot she got, she wouldn't move, just sighed gently to herself, which was funny and sort of lovely. In the evenings, other campers came and sat by her in their fold-up chairs and gave her a lot of fuss and bits of their leftover dinners, too. So she was happy enough.

I was happy, too, mostly. Despite the shadow of the Job, and what lay ahead.

We were there three nights, and every morning John would tramp down the narrow lane to the sea, where he'd strip down to his pants and go wading into the freezing cold tide. He'd never ask if I wanted to go, he'd just get up quietly first thing and I'd hear him pull on his boots, and once he was outside he'd let out that groan of his. The muntjac groan. And with my head pressed to the groundsheet I'd hear him walk across the grass, hear the vibrations of his army boots in my head, off and off he'd go until he reached the tarmac, and then his footsteps would disappear and once he was gone I pricked my ears for the sounds of the wolves beneath the earth, turning over in their sleep, snoring like old men.

Sometimes when he was swimming I'd go into the shops. I wasn't fussed with the jet, it was the fossils and teeth I liked.

I went looking for a bear claw, because I had this idea that I could wear it on a string around my neck. I'd read in a book from the library that if you wore a bear claw around your neck it meant that you'd never be killed by a bear, like it was a good omen or something. A lucky charm. But the shops in the village only had shark teeth, and prehistoric fish pressed flat in these polished stones, and skulls, big ones like Tyrannosaurus rex that John said weren't real, but cheap plaster casts made to fool tourists out of their money. He said most of the real fossils they sold in shops were from China now, or Morocco.

'Kids younger than you dig them up in quarries and get paid bugger all, and then they send them over here to sell in tat shops,' he said.

'But there must be fossils here, too,' I said.

'In the slate on the beach, yeah. There's still some, if you're lucky.' He said it like I shouldn't bother with them, though, and one afternoon, when I said I might go looking for fossils in the rocks near the water, he told me to leave them where they were. 'They're not ornaments. They were living creatures once, like you and me. And how would you like it if one day in the future someone had you stuck on their mantelpiece, eh?'

I'd smiled because I thought it was a joke he was making. But when I looked, he was dead serious about it. He was getting all angry again about nothing, so I didn't mention my dreams about the bears, or the sleeping wolves I'd hear at night in the woods. There was a lot we didn't talk about, things I knew made John angry, mostly. And the list seemed to grow until you didn't know what was off limits and what wasn't. Sometimes I felt like he'd have been happy if we'd just got on with things in silence. But then all of a sudden, John would get on his high horse about something, and it would all come out, like a burst water tank.

But anyway, whether we said it or not, the Job was on both our minds, even when we were walking along the cliff path or sitting in a field, or drinking tea, or watching the lapwings dive in the sky and listening to their whoop and whistle. Over on the coast, the Job was all we thought about, really. With John it meant Gold and Stars, of course. It meant that croft on an island somewhere, and freedom. But in my mind the Job was all mixed up with Toomey and with Pain and Blood and Death, and it wouldn't be long before we found out who was right, I told myself.

I kept my fingers crossed real tight that it wouldn't be me.

NINETEEN

'WHAT IF THE phone's not working?' I said. This was on the last evening and we were on the long flats of black rock with the tide coming in. The air was cold, but we'd been walking so long, skirting the cliffs, that our blood was burning in our veins.

'There's another payphone on the other side of the library, remember?' John said. 'They won't both be out of use. Or you run to the bypass.'

The sun had already set, but I was bending down, trying to stare into the dark crab pools by the growing starlight. There were clouds and no moon, though, and anyway I wouldn't have known what to do with a crab even if I saw one. The last narrow stripe of daylight was low on the horizon, and John was just a silhouette against the inky blue sky now, and the pools were black and silver and shining. We were alone out there with the sound of the sea, and orange lights in the houses on the slopes above us flickering like so many distant stars.

The rocks underfoot were slippery with seaweed and I was trying to keep my balance. John said you could eat it – bladderwrack, common kelp and laver. Cooked up with potatoes, he said, no different than cabbage or spinach. But I wasn't so sure. Anyway, I was too busy trying not to slip and snap an ankle to think about my stomach.

I could hardly see my hand in front of my face, but I wanted to stay out there in the night as long as possible, because I knew tomorrow we'd be back in the woods, in the van. And I didn't want it to end, not quite yet. And I didn't mind if my feet got wet, or if I had to wade back to the village soaked through and frozen like a drowned rat. As long as I was with John.

'Tell us what to say again.'

'You just say you've seen a motorbike going really fast, dangerously fast, heading towards Leeds. And if no one does anything about it he'll kill someone.' John's voice sounded loud in the dark with nothing but the steady lap of water to compete, and maybe it was too loud to tell of plans of robberies and escape, but there was no one around to hear. We were as alone as two blokes could be. 'It's easy,' he said. 'Nothing to worry about. The important thing is it's a man on a motorbike going fast, in the direction of Leeds.'

'But how will I know that you've finished the Job?'

'I'll be timing it just right. The delivery's usually on the hour. It'll take me ten minutes maximum, then you call the coppers at quarter past the hour. I told you all this.'

He was right, he had told me. But every time I tried to go over it all in my head it would get confused or end up in the wrong order.

'I leave early morning, I do the Job, then you call the coppers and you get them looking in the wrong direction,' John said. 'It might not work, but even if it buys me just a few minutes, that'll be a blessing.'

The sky was just a thin thread of blue stretched out along the horizon now. Everything else was black. Everything apart from John's voice, which sounded like colours out here. Like those poems of his. Like fire. 'When it's over, I get rid of the bike and go to Benny's place. He's got an old banger for us. Then I'll pick you up and we'll head north.' Banger was a car, a motor, a getaway.

'To the island, yeah?' I said. 'To the croft.'

'Not straight away, no. That'll take time. But there's plenty of places on the border to camp for summer while we find a place we can buy.'

'What about the veg at the van?' I asked. 'Who'll look after the leeks and that?'

'Don't you worry about the leeks. Worry about following the plan, all right?'

'All right,' I said. Then I remembered what Mam had told me. 'Will there be a doctor up in Scotland?' I asked.

John didn't say anything right away.

I looked up, but I couldn't see him anywhere. All I could see were the tiny lights of the village against the black, like jewels hanging off a curtain, and a black gap in those lights that could have been John-shaped. I couldn't tell how far away anything was any more, and I got a bit frightened. 'John?'

'Why will we need a doctor?' he said.

'For your medication. You'll still be taking it, right?'

Just black then. And silence in the black, and no colours.

'Will you?' I said. I reached out a hand to steady myself as the sea lapped at my ankles. 'Shall we go back now, John?'

The water was so cold it bit at my toes. My boots were soaked through, and my jeans were getting splashed now. The tide was coming in quicker.

Where was John? Had he already buggered off? I didn't know whether to try to get back to the shore or to wait. I didn't want John to think I was a coward.

'John? You there?'

I took a step forward, and my foot slipped down between a couple of sharp rocks, scraping the skin off my shin, and making me cry out loud. All I could see were the lights of the harbour a long way away, and the night, and no John.

I couldn't believe he'd leave me like this, out here in the middle of the sea.

I called his name again, then waited a few more seconds, then: 'Bastard,' I said, not caring if he heard me or not.

Bastard.

I grabbed the top of the nearest rock with my right hand and pulled myself upright, high enough so my ankle was out of the water. I didn't know if I was bleeding or not, it was too cold to feel anything. I wasn't going to waste time finding out, either. I needed to get back to the shore any way I could.

I started making my way across the rocks, slowly at first, wary of falling down and cracking my head or getting pulled out to sea by a wave. Because it was deep now, each wave growing higher, and when a bigger wave came I could feel the tide drag at my knees, and at my waist. A real pull, like hands on my belt, on my thighs.

I fell again, heavier this time, and now the snow-cold sea was in my hair and running down my neck, under my coat, under my shirt. The shock-splash of it in my nostrils made my lungs freeze. I pulled my head up and groaned against the sting of salt, trying to breath, but there was cold all around with no rest from it.

And I couldn't see the village now or the lights. I just saw black and heard the noise of sea everywhere, clogging my ears and my eyes. A rushing noise everywhere.

Black cold. Freezing cold. With no way out.

'Here, on your feet.'

Suddenly John's hand grabbed my wrist, wrestling me upright.

'Come on.' Dragging me after him. Holding me hard until I could walk on my own, his fingers stinging on my bones. Another few seconds and I was sucking in gulps of air and taking long strides through the waves by myself. Then shale underfoot, then sand, then the rendered stone of the harbour. My face as hard and cold as plaster in the night.

'Bastard,' was all I could manage to say, as we trudged up the lane, back to our tent and back to safety. 'You're a bastard, John.'

TWENTY

I woke with Mol's breath on my face, and I pulled her close and hugged her.

John wasn't in the tent.

I'd spent the night crying, but they were angry tears not sad ones, and I'd woken up more tired than I had been when I got in my sleeping bag. The ground beneath had been full of noise, a stampede of hooves and paws under my head not letting my mind rest. I'd hung my wet clothes up near the outdoor heaters to dry overnight, and so I'd had to sleep with nothing on, and I was cold and I was shaking. And it wasn't just the cold that made me shake, but something else. Not anger, exactly. Not fear. Something else, something new.

Hate.

I hated John. I'd hated him before, of course, but this was different. It was real. It was a hate I didn't have the word for. More horrible than hate. I wanted to hold onto it, remember it and not let it go. I wanted to remember what he was and what he'd done to me. How he'd left me there alone in the night, to teach me a lesson, to scare me. Because that's what it was. All because I'd had the balls to bring up the pills. I wanted to keep hold of the hate like a pebble in my pocket, so I could take it out whenever I liked, and polish it and make it shine.

I didn't get up straight away. I'd thought about getting dressed quickly and going off with Mol, so that when he'd get back from his swim I wouldn't be here and he might get a fright finding the tent empty. And I thought maybe he'd get worried and think I'd got lost or kidnapped or something, and realise he did something bad and maybe he'd even be sorry for it.

But the problem was, if he happened to come back early and find me half-dressed that would be worse somehow than finding me still in my sleeping bag.

So I waited a bit.

And a bit longer.

When he still hadn't come back after an hour, I climbed up and looked out of the tent and saw that his gear was gone. And I realised then that John was never coming back.

TWENTY-ONE

'Hello?'

'Hello, who is this?'

'Is Sophie there, please?'

'Yes, who is it calling?'

'I need to speak to her.'

'Yes, but what's your name?'

'Tell her it's the lad from the caravan.'

Silence.

I'd found a payphone at the top of the village, outside a shop that sold newspapers and vegetables and bags of bread and other bits and pieces. This was later. Because it had taken me a while to work out what he'd done. Just leaving me here without saying anything. On my own. Me and Mol. He'd never done that before, not ever. But here I was. And so after sitting in the tent, holding my knees, thinking but not thinking, feeling but not feeling, I'd decided to get up and put on my clothes and my coat, and walk up to see if I could find a phone to use.

Not that I knew anyone's number, apart from Mam's. And I wasn't going to call her, not now. She'd been through enough worry with me and John.

First thing John did when I came to live in the van was take hold of my phone, and say, 'You won't be needing this,' and I didn't see it again. John never let me have a mobile, see, and his pay-as-you-go didn't have any numbers saved, and only had enough money on it to make a quick call to arrange a meeting. He worked off bits of paper blokes would give him, scrawled with nicknames and numbers you could hardly read. Funny thing is, the only one I knew was his. John's. Which was useless now, because it was him that had left me, gone off in the night without saying goodbye.

There was the business card the lawyer in Leeds had given me. Alan. I took it out and looked at it. But I didn't want to talk to Alan. I didn't like him. And anyway, what would he do? I couldn't see some fancy lawyer from Leeds driving out to the coast to pick me up. He was no better than Toomey or any of the other dodgy blokes who'd come sniffing around the van, just all Mouth and Money.

I shoved my hands in my pocket, remembering something. A sharp corner of card stuck into the flesh of my thumb. It was the card Sophie had sent me, all folded up and creased. I opened it and looked at the number she'd written in it in fine blue biro.

'Hello, who's this?'

'It's me,' I said, feeling stupid and shy all of a sudden. 'That Sophie?'

'Yeah, hi.' A pause in her voice, uncertain. 'Sorry about my mother. She answers my phone like it's hers. So embarrassing.'

'It's fine,' I said. 'No bother.'

'So . . .' Another pause.

'I got your card,' I said. 'It's nice. Thanks.'

'Oh, you're welcome. Did it just arrive? I sent it nearly a week ago.'

'No,' I said. 'Yes, I mean. I got it, but I didn't know whether I better call or not. But today—'

'Has something happened?' Sophie must have heard something in my voice. Clever. Nice. All of a sudden I felt like talking. I wanted to tell her about John and last night, and nearly drowning. But you don't grass on your dad, and you don't tell people your business. I knew that much.

'I need a lift,' is all I said.

'Oh, right. OK.'

'I'm a long way away and I can't get home. Can you come and get me?'

'Wait, I'll ask my mum. Where are you exactly?'

I told her the name of the village, and she disappeared from the phone for a bit. When she got back I could hear a smile in her voice. 'We can't get there before four, but my mum says to go wait in a café and drink something. Tea, something hot. She wants me to ask whether you're safe.'

I said yes, I'm safe, and I said thank you, and after a while of not knowing what else to say, I told her I was glad her mam had picked up, and then I put the phone down.

I didn't sit in a café.

John had left me the camping stove and I boiled some water, and made a flask of tea. Then I packed up the tent and my gear, and left it all by the communal patio. After that I walked down the coast, me and Mol. I made myself forget about John and the Job and Toomey, and Gold and Stars. I forgot it all and just took in the sea and birds, and breathed the air.

We walked and walked, following the coastal path over hills of alum and clay, and down into soggy valleys of sleeping sheep where it smelled of slurry, through trees, and down onto beaches of shale. I watched the sunlight change its colours over the sheen of sea, and I watched the gulls swoop, and the distant shimmer in the water that might have been a dolphin or a seal. After a couple of hours, I sat in a field and drank my tea, and then I lay back and I thought about falling asleep.

Once the idea of sleep had come to me, it was like a switch was turned, and then I was sleeping, with my face warm with sun and the grass damp against my back, and I slept until it was time to head to the campsite again, and for the first time in months I didn't hear anything rumble beneath the earth, and I didn't dream.

In autumn, back in the van, acorns dropping from the oak would wake me. It spread high over the roof, twisted and rough as elephant hide, that tree, beautiful. And the clatter of the acorns, like pebbles on tin, would sometimes creep into my dreams while I slept, and rather than the wide-spreading oak tree, there standing above the van would be the stag with its antlers stretched out as long and pale as men's arms, dripping ticks from its tips, fat with blood.

I would picture it shake its broad skull and widen its eye, as though alert for some other great creature on the prowl. And then the rolling would begin, like thunder somewhere, and the stag would be gone, and the ground would shake and the van with it, and my bed and me.

I would lay there and listen to the forks and spoons clatter in the baked bean tin on the shelf, followed by the rattle of drawers, and the clash of glass water bottles set in rows on the sink. And outside there would be the slow scrape of hooves heavy against the mossy stone, and the creak of bowed branches, ash, beech and oak pressed open by the shaggy side of the thing as it came.

It was the bison, the one John had photographed.

Black and huge and unworldly.

And in my dream, I would wait, breathless, hoping against hope that it wouldn't linger but move on, back into the shadows, back where it belonged. But knowing all the while it had come here for me. Come to stare in through the little window and glimpse my face, and for a huge beast it was patient and still and it would not leave until I opened my eyes to acknowledge it.

But how to look at a thing like that and not go mad, I thought. Because maybe that's what had done for John. Not the bombs in the dirt and the sniper fire, but the ancient beasts that wouldn't let his mind rest. And if I opened my eyes and looked at it, his madness would become mine, too. And then who would look after him?

These were the thoughts that I spun back then, childish thoughts. And so I never did open my eyes, not in my dreams.

But later, when finally the things of the woods showed themselves, I would have no choice. And I would look at them, and whatever followed would follow.

TWENTY-TWO

Sᴏᴘʜɪᴇ, ᴡʜᴇɴ ꜱʜᴇ came, came in a blue Volvo.

Her mother parked it on the slope of road where all the bed and breakfasts were, and I waited while her and Sophie walked down the hill to meet me. Mol hobbled to them and turned her head to be stroked, eyes closed and as close to grinning as a dog can come. Sophie's mum was wearing jeans and trainers and a jumper, and her hair was dark and messy and she didn't look anything like Sophie who was pale and had freckles all over her face. Her mum frowned at me – that's what I thought anyway – then she bent down and petted Mol, politely, while Sophie came to talk to me.

'Your mam doesn't look happy,' I said.

'No, she's fine, just tired. The move has taken it out of her.'

When you have to keep secrets like me, you hear good lies everywhere, white lies. The kind Mam told me to keep me sweet when John was playing up. You get white lie radar. And mine was picking up the lie in Sophie, trying to make me feel better, to take away my guilt. But it was plain enough in her mam's face.

'Are you cold?' Sophie asked. Which I thought was a funny question, because I had my coat on, and in the sun I felt pretty warm, too hot, in fact. So I didn't get what she was on about, but now I know it's because I looked dead white when she saw me. Like I was in shock or something.

Before I could even thank her for coming, she turned back to her mother and said, 'We're just going to walk a bit. Won't be long.' And the unquestioning way her mother just nodded and carried on fussing over Mol made me see that it was something they'd discussed together long before they'd arrived. And that made me feel better somehow, because Sophie had been thinking about me.

'I'll be at the car,' Sophie's mam said, scratching Mol's chin. She tried to smile, and was doing a pretty good job of it for someone who was clearly hating being here. 'You two explore. She'll keep me company.'

'Where's your dad?' Sophie said, while we walked across to the campsite. 'Did you come here on your own? Mum says we should call him, make sure you have somewhere to go tonight.'

'He was here with me, but he had to leave,' I said, afraid to look in her eyes unless she saw through my lie as easily as I'd seen through hers. 'He had business, sort of an emergency. Tell your mam I'm fine, really.'

Sophie nodded. 'What were you doing here?'

'Just a break.' I shrugged. 'John wanted to come. It's nice here,' I said, adding, 'I could live here.' It came out without me wanting it to, or even thinking about it. But it was true. I liked the sea and beaches. It was different from the woods. In the trees, you felt closed off from the world, safe. Everywhere you looked there were shadows and bark, and the calls of birds echoing about. And there was the history that you could feel vibrate beneath your feet, skulls and bones deep down and all those things stirring. You could hide from people and the world there. But here when you looked out across the water, it looked like for ever. And the only noise was the waves and the wind.

'Me and my folks used to come here when I was little,' Sophie said. 'My gran used to live nearby in East Ferry. We rented a cottage down near the bay, and once we saw a film crew making a movie. We sat watching it all happening, and got quite close to the actors. It was a period film.'

'What's a period film?'

'It was set in the past,' Sophie explained. 'Like Victorian times.'

We'd stopped outside the reception place, no more than a cabin, where I'd left my gear. I felt awkward looking at Sophie's face, so I kept looking out to the sea, but every now and then I'd look across to the road to see if Mol was following us.

'She'll be OK. Mum's very good with dogs,' Sophie said, reading my thoughts. 'You know, you can talk to me, if you like. About anything,' she added.

I pretended I didn't hear. 'We haven't been apart for weeks,' I said, meaning Mol. 'Ever since I got her.'

'You love her?'

I didn't know how to reply, I'd never thought about it. She was just my dog. But I couldn't imagine being without her now.

'Yeah, I suppose,' I said, glancing to Sophie's face. She was looking up at the sky, so I let myself stare at her profile for a bit. A long nose, small mouth, hair falling over her forehead.

'Is he in trouble?' Sophie asked, without looking at me. Gulls were circling high up, floating like rags, bright as raw bone.

'Who?'

'Your dad.'

'John.'

'Yes, John. Is he in trouble?'

I didn't say anything for a while. I wasn't sure where to start, and maybe if it had been only Sophie and me then I might have told her. But there was her mother with Mol, waiting to drive us back, and getting more hacked off with me by the second.

So I never did reply to her, not properly. I just said, 'He's not well, not always.' And added, 'We better go.'

Then there was the journey back across the moors, with me and Mol in the back of the Volvo, while Sophie and her mother listened to old music on the radio, and Sophie leaning over the back of the seat every now and then, to see if I was OK. It was all a different world to me, all strange. Not bad, exactly. In fact, it was good being in their car, overhearing their daft talk and jokes that only they understood. I liked the calm and the silliness and noise and all of it, really. It's just, it wasn't my life, was it? And John was somewhere out there, but God knows where and God knows what he was doing or if he was even thinking about me. He was dead for all I knew. Dead and buried by Toomey or one of his henchmen, and if he was, I'd never know about it, I told myself, and never find the body.

And I thought, maybe it was over, and maybe I was free, and maybe this was my life now, or could be. All the while knowing it couldn't be true.

TWENTY-THREE

'WHY DON'T YOU come have dinner with us, and then we can take you back to your mother's place?'

This was Sophie's mam, once we were past York. After she'd given me the third degree about had I a responsible adult to care for me, what about school, was I well or should I see a doctor, do you think? It was dark now, and I didn't recognise where we were.

'Or you could sleep over,' Sophie added, smiling at me over the top of her seat. 'Can't he?' She looked to her mam, who said nothing. 'Does your mum know you're coming back tonight?' Sophie asked.

'No.'

I hadn't even thought about calling Mam or warning her, and I felt guilty all of a sudden.

'Then come over and stay the night. You can have a bath and a good sleep and we can drop you off tomorrow. Can't we? Mum?'

Sophie's mother nodded, sort of stiffly.

'No, I better go back tonight,' I said. 'She'll worry.'

Sophie didn't argue but I could see she didn't understand.

'Just dinner, then,' she said, and now I couldn't say no. She was like that, Sophie – she was kind and thoughtful, but when she had an idea, she didn't let it go. I suppose we were the same in some ways.

We arrived at their place before seven p.m. A light above the garage showed a red brick house, but big, with a wide gravel drive and privet hedges that lined closely mowed lawns, flat as concrete. It wasn't as big as the footballers' mansions me and John scouted, but it was big enough and it was posh, and it told me that whatever money problems Sophie's dad had, they'd get through them all right. But I doubt he was the kind to have ever lived in a caravan, and John would have said it just went to show that some people just aren't made for sorting proper problems.

I'd never been in a posh house before, and I ducked my head as I walked inside, as though the gravity might be different in there, or the air heavier. I didn't like to touch anything, in case I broke it or made it dirty.

I suddenly realised how mucky my hands were, and my clothes.

'Is Mol all right?' I asked, as she padded onto the carpet of the front hall with her dark paws, like she didn't have a care in the world. When I said it, Mol looked up at me, as if to say we were both in the same boat here. 'Coming inside, I mean.'

'Of course,' Sophie said.

'Her paws might be dirty, though. I don't want to be any bother.'

'It's fine, don't worry, the place is still a mess from the move anyway,' Sophie said, looking at me very steadily, like there was something else she was wanting to say but her mouth, her mind wouldn't let her. Something more than what was in her words. She glanced down at Mol's dirty paws. 'Mum won't mind, just let me talk to her.'

I looked at the warm electric light coming from the kitchen at the far end of the hall, where Sophie's mum had already disappeared, with Mol jogging after her, expecting food.

The light in the hall seemed very bright, and I couldn't help feeling like I was being watched, trapped somehow. 'Is there a loo I can use?' Loo being the posh word for bog, for gents, for crapper.

'Yes, of course. There's one down here, past the kitchen. But you can use the one in my room, if you like. There's a shower, too. I'll show you.'

'In your bedroom?'

She led me up the stairs, and into her room that smelled sweet and clean, like someone had just run a bath. I'd never known anyone with a shower in their bedroom. It didn't seem right.

Her bed was big and covered in cushions and pillows, and was the colour of cornflowers. It was spread around the room, her stuff, all random, and there were more boxes of things in the corner that she hadn't had time to unpack yet. There was a keyboard on a metal stand in the corner, a big TV fixed to the wall, a guitar, a drawing desk, a nightlight shaped like a star, and against the ceiling were shapes of butterflies, dozens of them, cut out and pasted up. And not picture-book butterflies, but real ones that you could identify.

Clouded yellow. Duke of Burgundy. Monarch. Orange tip. And brimstone.

'Do you like butterflies?' I asked.

She looked at me, a quiet, slow look. 'Moths and butterflies, yes,' she said.

I nodded.

'Here,' Sophie said, opening the door of a wardrobe and handing me a big, folded towel. 'Feel free to have a shower, take your time. Dinner won't be for half an hour, at least.' She seemed shy when she said it, and I didn't look at her. I just held the towel in my hands and bowed my head.

'Right, yeah,' I said. 'I must stink.'

'No, not at all,' Sophie said, 'I just want you to feel at home.'

It sounded like she was telling the truth, but this wasn't home, I wanted to tell her. Home didn't have showers in bedrooms. Home didn't have butterflies on the ceiling or towels so thick you could lose your fingers in them. Home was Mam's house, or the van. This wasn't anywhere like home. This could never be home.

'He's not a bad man,' I said, then. 'John.'

Sophie nodded, not knowing what to say. She was about to leave, then thought better of it. 'Why are you living with him? Why aren't you with your mum?' she asked. 'You've never told me.'

I was about to give her a lie, one of those simple ones that were easy to believe if you said it just right. But I didn't want to. Not any more, not with her. We were sitting on her bed, the clean towel folded in my lap. My fingers looked black bright against it, I thought. A labourer's hands, a wild boy's hands. And Derby's words came back to me: the Wild Boy of the Woods.

'He was in the army. Iraq, then Afghanistan. In the desert, John saw things happen. Bombs and things like that, killings. Bad things that stuck with him. He brings all that wherever he goes, he brought it home, back to our house, and it wouldn't let him be.' I looked at the towel while I talked, in case I saw her feeling sorry for me. I couldn't take that. Not from Mam, and not from her. 'The first time it happened, he was asleep and dreaming, and suddenly there was a bang, and when we got to the bedroom, he was starting up and shouting and yelling, like something was on him. Like he was having to fight them off. But he was asleep, too, see. And Mam tried to stop him but he just threw her off like she was nothing. And it was me then, and I didn't know what to do so I just tried to grab him and hold on.'

Sophie, she didn't say anything, just sat there in silence on the bed.

'Mam was screaming at him, but the thing was, he didn't push me away. Instead he clung onto me, and he was saying things. A name I didn't know. A boy's name, a boy he'd known in the desert. Later, he told us about him, some local kid who hung around the barracks, doing little jobs for a bit of money. A good kid, John said, always cheerful. The soldiers saw him as a mascot, a lucky charm. But one day he stood on a landmine, and it was John that found him, held him . . .' I realised I hadn't taken a single breath while I'd been talking, and I looked down and Sophie's hand was on mine, squeezing it tight. I looked up, and she was crying.

'So you see, he isn't a bad man. He's my dad,' I said. 'Just my dad.'

TWENTY-FOUR

AFTER WE'D EATEN, I let Mol out into their back garden to pee, and Sophie and me stood under the stars, while her mam glanced at us occasionally through the patio windows, suspicious, but quiet about it. I don't know where Sophie's dad was and didn't ask. Working, making the money for this place, I imagined.

It was warmer than the night before and the sky was clear as water, with the moon out, full and milk-pale.

'The police want him, don't they?'

Sophie had said it so gently that she might have been asking me what my favourite colour was, or where I went to school.

'Why do you say that?'

'Do they?'

'There's a job he's going to do,' I said, before I had time to stop myself. I hadn't wanted to admit it because it would have been grassing and John wouldn't let me squeal like that. But John wasn't about any more, I thought. He'd left. And it felt good, just saying it out loud, like I'd had this thing inside me, heavy and aching, and I could finally let it go.

'An army job?' Sophie asked.

I shook my head. 'Another sort of job, a big one. He's been working for a Bad Man called Toomey, who has something over John. He came to the van once, and I didn't like him. And this man, this Toomey, he wants John to do a job for him to pay him back, and John hasn't got a choice, because if he says no, Toomey will do something to him, or me. So John has to rob someone, and then he'll be free of his debt, he says.'

It all came out at once, and I'm not sure she understood straight away. It was a lot to take in, and I was talking fast. All that stuff that had been filling my head for weeks was finally out.

'A robbery? You mean, like a bank robbery?'

'Something like that,' I said, not wanting to say more. Truth was like a tick, I thought, and I didn't want it to attach itself to her, unless it did her harm. 'I think it's going to happen soon.'

'How soon?'

I shrugged.

'Does your mother know?'

'I can't tell her. I can't tell anyone.'

'You've told me.'

I said nothing to that. What could I say? I couldn't tell Sophie that I thought I loved her. I mean, it was stupid, I knew that. I hardly knew her, but the truth was she was the only thing I wanted right now, the only thing in the world that wasn't rotten and hopeless. 'You won't tell anyone,' I said. 'You can't. Please.'

She took hold of my hand.

We both looked at the night.

'Is it true that all the stars we see in the sky are dead?' I said, remembering something I'd heard. Something he'd said once. I'd been thinking about death a bit, I suppose. Not that I expected it to come to me or John, not really, but there were all those creatures under the ground and they must have been dead once, I thought. In the same way that they must have been alive once, and would be alive again. 'They say stars are so far away and their light takes so long to get to us, by the time we see it most of them have already faded and died.'

Sophie looked up. 'Some of them, I think,' she said. 'But not many. Most are quite close, only eight light years away.' She stared down to Mol. 'What do you think happens when you die?'

'John says nothing. He says there's nothing after you die, but that maybe in the few seconds when you go from living to dead, maybe to you that moment lasts minutes or hours or weeks, and you see whatever it was you wanted to see.'

'Like what, exactly?'

'Like a Hindu'll see an afterlife and reincarnation and karma,' I said. 'And a Muslim will see gardens of paradise. That's what he says, and it seems right enough.'

'You talk a lot about him,' Sophie said.

'He's my dad.'

'Yes. But what do you think?'

I toed the tip of my boot in the damp grass, and I thought for a bit. 'Me, I'd like it to be a forest, like in the old times. I'd like that when you die you go to a world where there was nothing but trees and plants and birds and butterflies, and we're as free as them.'

I could feel Sophie looking at me, the heat of her gaze making my face warm.

I shrugged. 'I don't know,' I said. 'I've not thought about it.'

'No, I like it,' she said. 'It's hard, isn't it?' she said, after we'd both been quiet for a bit.

'What?'

'Not knowing where your home is, or where you fit in.'

I didn't know what she meant right then, but now I know she was talking about being adopted.

'Mam's home is home,' I said. 'What about you?'

'This place, now,' Sophie said, glancing back to the window, to the glare of light and the slight figure of her mam behind the glass. 'But your caravan – what's that, then?'

'The van's where he's happy, that's all.' I shrugged. 'So I suppose I have two homes, haven't I?'

She glanced back to the house, then she looked to me and she nodded. 'If you still want to get to your mum's place tonight, we better go soon,' she said. 'Here,' she added, and quietly put a mobile in my hand. She'd had it in her pocket all this time. 'It's my old one. I don't need it any more. But it's got twenty pounds on it, and I've put my number in the contacts. Call me tomorrow and we'll meet up, OK? We'll try to come up with a plan together, to make it right.'

I looked down at the phone, my face astonished and dumb. Then I put the mobile in my pocket. 'I haven't got anything to give you,' I said. 'It was your birthday and I never gave you a thing.'

'The blackbird's nest,' she said. 'You gave me that.'

'Don't be daft, it's not the same. You can't give something just to look at.'

'You can, you did,' she said. 'And you'll show me more. I know you will, so take the mobile and take my thanks, too, in advance.'

I didn't argue. Even then, I didn't know what I was going to do, not really. I thought I'd just stay with Mam, like I'd said, stay there and see if he ever got in touch. Then maybe see Sophie and we'd plan what to do next – stay away from the woods maybe, go back to school. But you don't know when ideas will take over you, or why. Not always. And maybe it was thinking about the boy in the desert, maybe it was that . . .

Sophie's house smelled powdery and clean, and later, once her mother had driven me to the estate, to Mam's house, and when I was getting out of the car and getting ready to knock on the door, the smell of Sophie's soap and shampoo was still there, clinging to me.

I was hoping her mam would drive off as soon as I got to the front path, but she just waited for me to go safely inside. The windows of the house were all dark, which meant Mam was doing a late at the nursing home. You lucky sod, I told myself. So I dumped my camping gear in the garden, then bent down to get the spare key from beneath the plant pot by the drain, waved to Sophie's mam and unlocked the door.

I stood in the porch until I heard the car pull away. As soon as it turned the corner, I backed down my mam's path, and walked onto the street, down past town, and when I got to the river I headed into the woods again, where the wolves were already waking up . . .

PART THREE

TWENTY-FIVE

WHEN I GOT to the caravan, it was still inky dark, night dark, and there was a black breeze making the bare branches overhead sway. There was no light on in the caravan, so I kept quiet crossing the stream and climbing up to the front door. It must have been overcast with no moon, because I didn't see the yellow and black tape wrapped all the way around until I got right up to the step. But I heard it clapping in the wind. I'd heard it all the way from the fields, without knowing what it was.

CLAP, like the sound of crow wings.

CLAP CLAP.

Derby.

I'd forgotten all about him, forgotten to tell John, and now he'd done what he'd threatened to do. The caravan had been condemned, notices plastered up all over it, yellow paper in plastic envelopes and a great big hazard notice made out of tin that warned to *KEEP CLEAR*. The windows had been broken in, and Derby or whoever he'd paid to wreck the place had even gone so far as to smash a great hole in the roof. You could see the ceiling hanging down like wet paper through the broken-in windows. Someone had gone to work on the sink and the cupboards with a hammer, too.

I looked around for John, or any sign of John, but no one could live or sleep in the place now. Anyway, Derby had fitted a chain round the door with a padlock as big as a fist, just to make sure.

I went back to the stream, and sat down on a rock. I felt empty, sort of frightened. But there was a fire inside me, too. Nothing like the hate I'd felt before. It was more like excitement. I'd come here out of habit. Muscle memory, John called it. Back to what I knew. But it was more than that. It was because I still owed it to John, to not let him down, to look after him like I'd done before, see that he didn't get killed or banged up again or worse. Because I'd promised Mam, and I'd promised him, too.

And God. But not in words.

But with the caravan all kicked in, then what was to stop me giving up and going back to Mam's and living like normal again? I'd done my best, I thought, so why couldn't I have my old life back?

I'd go back to school again, I thought. Not that I was looking forward to that, because I never did get on too well there. And not just because of Otley, or the teachers. I just didn't get on. But I'd go back to school anyway, and at the weekends I'd meet up with Sophie, and me and her and Mol would go on walks, and she would teach me more butterflies, and I'd tell her what wild plants are good to eat, and she'd tell me about the stars and the universe. And Mam and me would be all right, too, and if John was around then maybe he'd get a proper job. And I'd be working soon, because school wouldn't go on for ever, after all.

I sat there and I let my mind go on like that for a while, daydreaming at first. Then proper dreaming.

I was tired, and I must have nodded off sitting there, and all those thoughts about the future swam in and out of my head. They were joined by the soft sound of the stream bubbling away by my feet, and there were other noises, too. There were rocks grinding underground, old graves opening up like mouths. I heard beasts wake and yawn. Beasts as big as buses, all horns and teeth with fur sharp as broken glass. Wolves and bears and bison lumbering up, wanting free. They shook their coats and the soil fell from their backs in great wet clods that made the trees tremble down to their roots, and scared the birds into the sky.

I saw a whole world right there, an ancient place where we didn't belong. A place that was better without us. It was a green place, and dark, but there were no wars or bullies or gangsters or robbers. Just the beasts and trees and insects and the birds above them all.

And not a single gun.

I was still dreaming when I heard John's voice, and I didn't know if he was in the dream or out of it.

'You didn't bother to tell me,' he was saying.

I blinked my eyes open.

'You didn't bother to tell me.'

He was moving to me through the trees in long strides, his face screwed up in anger, yelling.

'What the bloody hell's wrong with you, lad, eh?'

I managed to stumble up to my feet as he reached out. 'What are you on about, John?'

He was on me quick, his big hands grabbing my arms, pulling us face to face. And I saw this desperate look there, like a drowning man. Like before, the bad times when Mam would have to call the police on him.

'The van. That's what I'm on about.'

'I'm sorry,' I said. 'I forgot to tell you. I'm sorry, John.'

'You're sorry?' He shook me, hard. 'What good is sorry now?'

'What's happened?' I asked.

I knew about the van. I knew about Derby getting shot of us. But this was different. John was scared, and he didn't scare easy.

His hands loosened on me.

'You don't understand,' he said.

'Tell me,' I said.

He let me go and stepped back, his head down. His boots were in the stream, water sloshing over his ankles. He was wearing the same gear he'd had on at the coast. His jeans were caked in mud, and his coat was torn at the shoulder.

The clouds broke open, and the moonlight shone so dim and blue it looked like the woods were underwater, and us with them.

So maybe we were drowning, I thought. Me and John. Drowning, never to recover.

The trees were no more than narrow bars set black against the night, but there was a fog of light around John. It flickered and splashed up from the lap of water beneath. I could see that his hands were shaking, and his knuckles were red and raw. Bruised.

'John?'

'No, I'm sorry,' he said, his voice low. 'This is my mess.'

'John, have you been in a fight? Who was it? Was it him? Has Toomey been?'

John just tipped his head up and looked at me, and he didn't have to answer. I knew the truth. I could smell it standing around us like the dim dark, and the trees and the ghosts of those beasts.

Pain and Blood and Death was here.

And its name was Toomey.

TWENTY-SIX

'D<small>O YOU BELIEVE</small> it?' Sophie asked, the next morning, on the phone, when I told her I was back with him, and told her that as far as I knew the Job was off now. 'About the fight?'

'I don't know what to believe. John doesn't lie. Hang on—' I was whispering, keeping my voice down, because John was still asleep. We'd lugged what we could across the woods, away from the van where Toomey's men would be looking for us, and down under the railway bridge half a mile away, where we'd done our best to get some kip.

Kip meaning sleep, meaning doze, meaning shut-eye.

I walked down the dirt track, far enough away from where John was lying that I was confident I was out of earshot. 'Sorry,' I said. 'You still there?'

'You said he saw things, didn't you?' Sophie continued. 'Like bulls? So how can you trust what he says?'

She meant the bison and the bear and the wolves, because I'd told her the history of the woods as John knew it. The mythology. I'd trusted her. But what I hadn't told her was that I'd seen them, too. That I'd heard them at night, and when I woke in the dark I could smell their fur and their hide, and I knew they'd been.

'He's not imagining Toomey. I met him, remember?'

'But – how much money was he talking about, exactly?'

'It wasn't about the money with him,' I said. 'It was about escape.'

'But it sounds so dangerous. You shouldn't have to deal with thieves and criminals like Toomey. What if John's made things worse?'

There was no doubt he'd made it worse, I wanted to tell her. But at least now the robbery wasn't going to happen, was it? So I just said, 'Yeah, but he understands men like Toomey. He knows what makes them tick.'

Here I was defending him again, it's all I ever did. It's all I knew.

'Sorry,' Sophie said, and I told her she said sorry too much. And she said sorry back. And we laughed. And now the tension was gone again, just like that, and we were back like we wanted to be. Because she had the trick, did Sophie. A trick John had never learned, and me, neither. The trick of knowing when to stop.

John had this thing he used to say.

'If you want to know what kind of life you should lead, then first you need to know what kind of person you are. It's the only duty any of us has, and one most of us, the weak especially, ignore. It's the reason we're all here, and if by the time we're done with this life and we know who we are, and we can say we're proud of what we did, then that's enough. Don't be weak, lad, for God's sake,' he'd end up telling me. 'Weak men are death to this world.'

This was when I'd just arrived at the caravan, when John knew who he was, or seemed to. He'd stopped crying and shouting by then. Whatever had been in him since the desert had settled and calmed, gone quiet. Those wolves had fallen asleep, and moss had grown over them.

I thought they'd gone altogether. But now something had changed. I could hear the boy in his voice again, like Mam used to call it when she was scared for him. The boy in the desert.

A boy in the dark, looking for a way home.

'Did you kill him?' I asked, once I'd ended the call with Sophie and was back under the bridge. I meant Toomey. Because that's what I saw in my head – Toomey face down somewhere, dead as a doornail and bloody with it. 'John, tell me.'

He was still curled up on the ground, amongst the rubble and ferns, awake but eyes like cracks and white spots in his cheeks that made him look half mad. He'd slept right through, no moving or talking, no shaking, while I watched over him.

'John,' I said. 'Did you?'

'No, but I should have done.'

'Is he in a bad way?'

'He'll live.'

'Will he come after us?'

John nodded. He'd told me enough last night to get the picture, but now he told me more – how in anger he'd gone to see Toomey to tell him it was over, that he had no intention of committing the robbery and repaying whatever debt he owed. This was after he left me at the coast, in the campsite. Something had changed in him, he'd said. Looking at the sea, with me. He knew he couldn't do it any more, not for men like Toomey. And he told me how it had ended in a fight between him and Toomey, a bad one, with John beating him down in his own house, by the swimming pool. Blood in the blue.

'What'll happen now?'

'Nothing good, unless we get going. I'll need to be on the road, head for Scotland, like we'd planned.'

'So the Job – it's over, right?'

He propped himself on his elbow and began to scrabble around with his hands, checking what gear we had. John had smashed into the van, and we'd saved what we could, what hadn't been torn up, which wasn't much. But at least Derby's blokes hadn't found the tool box under the van, or the sawn-off. It was here now, in John's holdall, safe and sound.

'John?' He was taking too long to answer, I thought. I didn't like it. 'Well, is it?'

'We'll do a different job.' He looked at me, his face a question, like his answer had surprised even him. 'Similar plan, but it'll be Toomey's money we nick and plenty of it, and not Hazlit's. That all right?'

I didn't understand what he was saying, so I just nodded, but with no enthusiasm.

John saw as much. 'I'll need you onboard with me, yeah?'

'Yeah, course,' I said, without knowing what I'd agreed to. 'But do I still have to call the coppers?'

'That's right, but this time Toomey's men will be looking for us, and they're not stupid and they're not old, so we have to be extra careful. I know their timings – the money collection, the security vans. I say we get on with it as quick as we can. Tomorrow's best.' He was talking as much to himself as me, working through the possibilities out loud and leaving me in the dark. 'Toomey launders money through his betting firm, black money passed from shop to shop. I've helped him with it. Tomorrow he has a delivery over in Granthorpe, not thirty minutes away. But he doesn't use security vans. He has his own heavies, they drive big shiny bastards. SUVs, like they're in Los Angeles.'

I let him talk, not knowing what he meant half the time, but dreading each word. Sometimes you just had to let him go on, because if you didn't those thoughts festered in him, boiling up until they had to break loose. Like they had with Toomey the night before.

'If we sort ourselves out today, get some food in us, then make sure we get a good kip tonight, we can get it done and over by tomorrow afternoon,' John said. 'But we can't sleep here, it's not safe.'

'Where, then?'

We marched back, trailing the woods, not down the railway tracks but the other way, out to the industrial estates where the lorries would park up overnight before going back onto the motorway. We found a spot fifteen feet behind the fence in the thick of some young birch, and cleared the ground of Coke cans and bottles and crisp packets, then stashed our gear, before walking to the burger hut. John bought tea for both of us, a can of lemonade and two pies each, one for breakfast and one for later. Then we headed for the canal, where we'd spend the day, he said, away from prying eyes. All the while my head was spinning, trying to catch up with John's thoughts – the way he saw things.

What's funny is it was sort of nice, being there. And if it hadn't been for tomorrow waiting for us, and the Job, then it would have been one of the best days in months. John got a bit of twine from his coat pocket and made a sort of fishing rod out of some willow, and handed it to me while he made a second for himself. And we sat there, just staring at the sun on the water, and we didn't say anything and we didn't mind if a fish bit or not. It was only later that I realised we didn't even have a fly or a hook on our lines, so no way were we going to catch anything. But we just sat and waited and watched and felt the time leak away, and with it went the tension of the night before, until we both decided to lay ourselves down by the hedge and nap.

A few hours in, John said he was off to collect the bike from Benny for tomorrow, and I went back to sleep and dreamed of the woods again. But this time the wolves were far away, howling, and the stars were out and shining bright, and Sophie's voice was in my ear, mapping them out for me.

When me and John and Mol made it back to the lorry park, it was still light, but we bedded down anyway. John slept on the bare ground and gave me his sleeping bag because mine was still at Mam's. He didn't bother to hang up a screen or cover. No one looked this way and, anyway, John said that all the lorry drivers parked on the estate would be in their cabins soon, fast asleep or drunk.

'Will she be quiet?' he asked, staring into Mol's silvery eyes.

I patted her gently on the nose. In the last few days she'd walked more than she'd ever walked, and she was already closing her eyes and bedding down for the night.

'She'll be quiet,' I said. 'Are you going to tell me what happens tomorrow?'

John didn't look at me. He just pulled his hat low over his eyes and folded his hand under his head. 'Get some sleep. It'll be an early start.'

But I couldn't sleep for the noise of the engines ticking over, and the flash of floodlights in the branches, so I turned in my sleeping bag and took out the mobile and I saw Sophie's name.

Goodnight, she'd texted. *Sweet dreams*.

Then I put it away and I just listened to John snore, and as I worried Mol's fur with my fingers I tried to ignore the ache in my stomach that felt like Death coming closer.

'Up. Come on.' John's voice woke me. Sun and birds and the noise of traffic nearby.

He was already packed and ready, and I wondered why he hadn't got me up earlier. Mol was crouched low nearby and shaking, having her morning pee.

'Get your things,' John said, dragging the sleeping bag off my legs, as I pulled myself up. I'd slept with all my clothes on and I could smell the oil from the road on my skin, and sweat, and morning earth. Ten minutes later and we were up and walking back through the trees to the patch of cement where John had left the bike yesterday.

And suddenly, without me thinking about it, the Job was on. It was the day it was all going to go wrong, and the thing is, I half knew it. Even as I was packing up my bag and as we ducked through the fence, I knew. Maybe I'd always known, ever since John had come back from the war, ever since he'd walked out into the woods, I'd known how it would end.

I just didn't know when.

But now I tell myself that if I had really known all this, then I'd have run out into the road and never looked back, wouldn't I? Instead we went to the patch of poured cement and I looked at John and he looked at me, and we said nothing. We just looked. Then he hugged me and told me to remember – 'Fifteen after twelve, midday. In the direction of Leeds.' And I said I'd remember, and I told him I loved him and I watched him go, and stayed standing there until he was just a speck of nothing in the distance. Just a blur of noise.

Then I walked back into the trees.

TWENTY-SEVEN

IT TOOK ME nearly an hour to get to the town centre. John had left me his share of gear to carry, and what with his kit bag and spare boots, I was sweltering by the time I got to the pick-up point, even though it was March. There was an abandoned petrol station with an overgrown common in front and fields at the back, and I hid the gear in a fenced-off timber hut behind.

We'd meet after the Job was over. He'd come after he'd picked up the banger, and get me and Mol, and we'd head north as quick as we could, camp a night or two while we gathered our thoughts and waited to see if the cops would be after us. Because if we were lucky they wouldn't even be called, he said. It would just be Toomey and his men who'd bother with us, and they didn't have anyone working for them past Newcastle. Once we got to the border, we'd be home clear. And John would get a job on the farms for summer, and me, too, if I liked, he told me. Saving cash, and scouting out a place to buy. That's what he planned. Simple as, he said. Best plans are simple and no bother. Just like lies.

Sophie's text came just after nine.

By that time I'd got to the public toilets in town. I'd had to wait until the bloke from the council came to unlock them. Then I'd had a proper wash, because I felt grubby after sleeping by the lorries. I cleaned my hair, too, and the water was cold, so I warmed my hands under the blower for five minutes. I didn't usually feel the cold too much, but I did that day. Cold and hot, like a fever about to burst.

Every clock I walked past in town, I'd check my watch against it, make sure it was the right time. I was dead nervous, and I didn't like it. Didn't like the unfamiliar feeling of my cold fingers and the blood in my heart going at a hundred miles an hour.

Are you around today? Sx

I didn't answer straight away. I didn't know what to say. I wanted to see her, course I did. But I couldn't think straight until the Job was over. How could my mind settle till I knew John was safe and we were free?

But I knew, too, that it would be a long morning if I just carried on wandering around the streets and looking at my watch. And anyway, John had told me not to show myself too much in town, and to keep my head down, just in case one of Toomey's blokes was out and about after what had happened.

And whatever you do, don't go to the caravan, he'd said.

No matter what.

Never go to the caravan.

I thought of heading to Mam's, just to pass the time. But what would I say to her? I couldn't tell her what John was up to or she'd call the coppers and then John would be banged up again and he'd hate me.

So if Sophie wanted to see me, there was no reason not to, I told myself. No reason at all. In fact, it would help me get off the streets, out of sight. And anyway, if I didn't see her now, when would I? Because once the Job was over – if it all came off as planned – we'd be gone, John and me. And when we were gone I'd probably never see Sophie again, because we'd be on the run, wouldn't we? We'd have to stay in Scotland, I thought. I'd never see Mam, not for a long time. Everything would change. Everything. Whether I liked it or not.

Maybe I hadn't thought about it all until then, not properly. Hadn't pictured what it would be like – our life together in Scotland, just us two. That's not what I wanted, of course. I wanted Mam there. But if she wouldn't go, then what could I do? You can't tell grown-ups. They do what they like no matter what. Doesn't bother them that they make you unhappy, ruin your life, break up homes and end stuff. It's like they can't help smashing things. It's their nature.

I don't just mean John and Mam. But all of them.

The ones that love you. The ones that hate you. All of them.

Something happens when you get past a certain age, something dies inside. It's not wars that do it, or boring jobs or not having money or any of that. It's something else. You see it everywhere. I saw it in Derby and in Toomey, and in all the shabby little men that came into the woods and did business and drove off, no happier after they came than before. They smiled and joked and mucked about, but not one of them was proper happy. The smiles had died before they even reached their faces. The ones in the flash cars and nice suits, especially. Even

Toomey. The only thing alive in him was greed and a desperate, clinging need to win.

I was glad John had given him a good hiding. People like that needed to be brought down a peg or two, I told myself. Not that it changed anything. Because that's the other thing with grown-ups. Mam was right, they don't change. Once they get like that, once they get fixed on whatever way of thinking they have, whether it's divorce or war or a robbery, you can't stop them.

I promised myself I'd never be like that. I'd promised myself a lot of things, living in the van with John. I'd promised I'd never fight or rob. I'd told myself I wouldn't be like him, that if I ever got married I wouldn't leave my wife, and I'd never treat my kids like he treated me. Not that he was bad, because he wasn't. I loved him. But he was just like the rest, that's all.

And I wanted to be better.

And once the Job was over, once we were gone, I would be.

I'd be good, I told myself.

And for the time the words existed in my head I did believe them.

TWENTY-EIGHT

S HE CAME AN hour after I texted. Just Sophie on her own, in a taxi. We met at the café by the main row of shops and she bought me a tea, insisting she paid. And because she was paying I didn't order anything to eat, even though I was starving. And if it had been me paying I'd have bought myself a bacon sandwich. But it wasn't, so I just sat and watched as Sophie ate a croissant, and drank her coffee.

'You're joking,' she said, angry at first when I told her the plan. 'You can't. You'll both get yourselves killed.' Then, when she'd had time to calm down a bit, she asked, 'This Toomey, apart from the betting shops, what does he do?'

I thought about it. I only knew what John had said, and I didn't know how much to believe – rumours about drugs, and blokes getting their legs broken and factories being burned down.

'He loans money,' I said. 'John says he owns half of this town, and property in Leeds, Bradford, Manchester.'

'Did he get John put in prison, do you think?'

I shook my head. 'I think he got him out.'

'I don't understand,' Sophie said, putting down her croissant. 'How do you mean?'

'Well, the lawyer John had, this Alan bloke, I think Toomey paid him. He hasn't told me, but I think Toomey got him off a longer sentence, and that's why John owes him. He was up for burglary, but suddenly he has this lawyer and then he's banged up for just trespass. So, you tell me.'

'Really? How do you know all this?'

'I don't. I'm guessing.'

A lot of what I was saying were just notions I'd come up with over time, putting two and two together. John was a closed book, and he'd never tell me a thing. Not if he thought it would put me in danger. But there had to be a reason why suddenly John had a private lawyer on his case, and why this lawyer gave him a sawn-off shotgun to store away, and why John would have anything to do with a man like Toomey in the first place. The way I saw it, Toomey had pulled some strings and got John off a more serious charge, and now he was trapped. And his way out was to rob the bloke of his own money, which was typical John. It matched his weird sense of justice. 'You have to turn the world upside down sometimes,' he'd told me once, and I thought he was repeating something from one of his books, something this William Blake had said maybe. But they were his words, just John.

You had to turn the world upside down.

And he meant it. He meant that sometimes the rules weren't enough, so you needed to break them, do the least logical thing, the stupid thing, because it was all that was left over when you'd rejected everything else.

That was the way he thought sometimes, and you couldn't tell him he was wrong.

'You need to call the police,' Sophie said, which was something I'd been waiting for her to say ever since she'd arrived. 'Even if your dad gets away with stealing from him, this Toomey will find you eventually. And when he does, how do you know he won't kill you and John? You say he's dangerous.'

'He is. But if John gets banged up again, it'll be for a long time. And it'll be my fault.'

'Isn't that better than him getting killed?'

I turned to look through the window, to where Mol was sitting by the bench outside. People were stopping to pat her, telling her what a good girl she was.

She wasn't the only thing out there.

Down the road, behind a big black car, there was a bloke standing looking towards the café. He was as wide as he was tall, and he was bald and wearing a leather jacket and blue jeans, and he was bad at not looking threatening. It wasn't Toomey's Range Rover, but it was definitely his style.

'Are you sure you don't want something to eat?' Sophie said. 'Hey, are you OK?'

I leaned back in my chair and out of the square light from the window. 'I need to go,' I said.

'But you've just got here.' Sophie looked at her watch. 'It's not even half past ten yet.'

'I've got to go,' I said.

Sophie turned in the direction of where I'd been looking. 'Is that him?' she asked, seeing the bloke.

'No, but I think it's one of his men.'

'Has he seen you?'

I couldn't know for sure. But the way he was standing there, very still, told me that he probably had. And if by any chance he hadn't seen me, then he'd definitely seen Mol. 'I have to go, I'm sorry.' I got to my feet and Sophie got to hers. She grabbed my hand and held it, and I felt the warmth of her fingers in mine. I wanted to stay, to talk, to spend the day with her and not go back to the world of guns and robbers and running away.

I wanted to tell her I'd like to kiss her.

But what I did is I squeezed her hand as softly as I could, then I pulled out of her grasp. I spilled some change on the table from my pocket, enough for my tea, then I said sorry one last time and I went out to Mol and hurried down the street.

TWENTY-NINE

IT WAS STUPID, I see that now.

There was nowhere to go, after all. If Toomey was onto me, then I couldn't make the call, and couldn't get to the pick-up point, and so the plan was over before it had begun. It was no safer out in the open than it was in the café. If I'd been thinking straight I could have asked Sophie to get her mam to come and pick us up. At least then we might have got somewhere safe until the time came to meet John. But I hadn't been thinking, which was always my problem. John knew that. It's why he'd have to repeat things over and over until I got it. About birdsong and forage food, and about the plan. The teachers knew it, too. Knew how slow I was, how hard it was to hammer the simplest things into my head. Because they thought I was thick, and maybe I was. But maybe my mind just raced in a different direction, I thought. Maybe life wasn't always about facts and numbers and getting the right answer. Sometimes it was about getting through a day alive, and so far I'd done a pretty good job of that.

I made my way past the shops and towards the library that gave out onto a little park. Mol tried to keep up as I ran into the bushes and followed the stone wall round the back.

'Here, girl,' I said, grabbing her neck and pulling her closer. If she'd have been brown or black, maybe the bloke wouldn't have seen us. But Mol was yellow and slow and easy to spot. And that meant I was easy to spot.

My mobile went off. Sophie.

Get ready to run.

I didn't understand, so I just waited. And then I saw the bloke in the leather jacket. He was on the other side of the road, looking our way, but casually, as though he was just out for a stroll. I could see him take his phone out of his pocket, and put it to his ear as he waited for the traffic to clear so he could cross. I imagined it was his boss he was calling. Toomey. Telling him he'd got hold of me.

That's when Sophie appeared.

She was looking nervously around, staring across to the park, and to us. She waved, quickly, then walked straight up to Toomey's heavy and started talking to him.

I couldn't believe it. Couldn't believe she'd do something like that, and for me.

Couldn't believe the courage it took.

The bloke looked annoyed, trying to wave her off. He knew what she was up to, and he was trying to keep his eyes on me and Mol, while at the same time looking for a break in the traffic. But Sophie wasn't having any of it. She started pulling at his sleeve. Then, when it was clear he still wasn't about to look at her, she started to scream.

Honest to God, screaming.

She was shouting out to anyone around that she needed help, that the bloke was hassling her. Which got him off his phone pretty quick, I can tell you. I watched as a small crowd of people started gathering around, and then, so quick no one would have noticed, Sophie glanced around to us as if to show me she was all right. She might even have smiled.

While the bloke was busy telling his story to the crowd, I climbed over the wall, and pulled Mol after me, and we jogged down the bank and onto the lane below, and broke into a run. I looked at the time. We still had long enough to put a good distance between me and Toomey's man and then double back the long way and get to the payphone in time for the call to the police.

I texted Sophie a quick thank you, then went down to the railway tracks.

The rest of the morning was horrible and slow.

Every few minutes I'd try to imagine where John was, and what he was doing. First thing was to check the banger was in place and the engine was running OK. Then at ten he'd have got to the betting shop in Granthorpe, to see that it had opened as usual. Then he had to make sure the collection vehicle arrived at each shop, sticking to the schedule. Toomey's collection was always made in the same order, he said – the shop in Denton, then the shop in Hockley and, lastly, the shop in Granthorpe. None of them were far away, but the route took about an hour in total. He'd wait on the Hockley road, until the car came by. It would be a black Mercedes SUV, easy to recognise. Once it arrived, John would follow it to the Granthorpe shop, and wait until Toomey's men came out with the cash. That's when John would hold them up. He'd carry a knife with him, too, so he could slash the tyre of the SUV, making sure it couldn't follow him. Then it would be down to him to get back to Benny's, swap the bike for the banger and head to the pick-up point, where he'd collect me and the gear, and we'd drive north, as far as we could go.

They wouldn't have expected it, the men. Who in their right mind would rob Toomey? It was Hazlit who had to be wary, after all. Hazlit who was stepping on toes. So they'd be shocked at first, maybe even amused, thinking the bloke on a bike might have something wrong with him, a screw loose. But the gun would convince them, then the slashed tyre, then the bike and the man on it riding off like he'd spent a lifetime robbing villains. And if by any chance, Toomey reported the robbery, I'd have already told the cops about a bloke riding like a madman on the way to Leeds.

I checked my watch.

11:02.

Ten minutes later, Sophie texted to tell me to be careful. She said she'd tried to keep Toomey's man as long as possible, but he'd got in his car and driven off, and he'd be after me again.

Then she'd texted just one word.

Sorry.

I didn't know then what she'd done. Or what it could mean. But a few minutes later, the mobile started buzzing. I looked at the number, and something about it looked familiar. I thought it might be Sophie calling on a different phone, so I answered.

'Tell me he's not doing something stupid.'

'Mam.'

For a minute I couldn't work out what had happened. I stared at the phone, trying to take it in. How had Mam got the number?

Then I realised why Sophie had apologised. For finding Mam's number, calling her, warning her.

'How d'you find me?'

'Lucky for you that girl has more sense than you'll ever have. For God's sake, what's happening?'

'Nothing.'

'Don't lie to me.'

'It's a job. He had no choice, honest.'

'What job? Where? Tell me what the hell he's got himself involved in.'

'It'll be over soon. Another hour and then we'll be gone. It's all planned out.'

'Stop it. Please, whatever it is, you have to stop it. If you ever want to see him again, just stop it. Do you understand? And don't get involved. Promise me you won't be involved.'

'I can't. He needs me.'

'I *need* you,' Mam said, howling down the phone so loud the signal seemed to crackle and fade. 'I need you alive and I need you safe. I can't lose you as well.'

'I'm all right, Mam. I promise, I'm fine.' As I said it I could tell that nothing would convince her, because she was right. It was stupid. The whole thing had been a disaster from the start. Why hadn't I tried to stop him? I could have tried, and I didn't.

But a man like John isn't stopped easily. I knew that.

A man like John doesn't listen. A man like John had seen too much, lived too much, known too much blood and hate and stupidity to be swayed in an argument. He'd do what he'd set out to do, and you were either with him or against him.

So that's why, I told myself. Because he needed someone, just one person who'd stand beside him. No matter how stupid it was. No matter how disastrous it turned out to be.

Only I wasn't beside him, was I? I was miles away, hiding down a lane, on the phone to my mam. What good was I to him now?

'I'll see he's all right,' I said. I didn't know how, but I meant it. Right then I meant it. And you can believe me or not, it doesn't matter any more. But I tell you that I did. And maybe Mam heard it in my voice, that certainty, because she seemed to quieten down then. And her voice, when she spoke, was clear and steady.

'I want you to listen. Are you listening?'

'Yes.'

'Whatever it is you two are involved in, I want it ended. Now. Whatever trouble he's in, we can work it out. However bad it is, there's a way out, and we can do it together. Do you hear?'

'I do, yeah.'

'I'm trusting you. I know it's not your fault. God knows none of this is your fault. It's your dad and me that's caused this mess, but I need you to help him out of it, OK?'

'OK.' A silence as deep as a well came down the line. 'I'm sorry, Mam,' I said.

'Don't be sorry, darling, be safe.'

THIRTY

I WAS HALFWAY BACK to the shops and the payphones when I saw the black SUV. It was cruising at the bottom of the high street, like it was ready for another turn around the town, on the lookout. I shrank into the stone of the nearby wall, my heart hammering hard. I felt it in my throat, the blood, and the hot rush of it in my ears made me dizzy. There was no way I could make it to the phones without being seen and caught. Not with Mol beside me, anyway. As long as I had her with me I couldn't stay out of sight. Any one of Toomey's men would spot me a mile off.

I looked at my watch again. It was almost time.

I wasn't going to leave Mol, so we had to get somewhere else, somewhere out of town. And the only place I knew was the woods. And all right, John had told me not to go anywhere near the van, but I wasn't thinking straight, those tiny feet pattering on my chest again. Anyway, I told myself, I didn't need to go near the van, did I? I knew the trees and the stream and the little quarry in the valley. I knew it better than any of Toomey's men. And it was a better place to meet than the petrol station, because that was too close to the town centre to be safe now that the SUV had taken up there.

So I ran.

I ran down the lane, down to the railway tracks and back to the woods. Down the familiar trails me and John had trod so many times before. Down the well-worn ruts roughed-up by our boots on moonless nights when it seemed like morning might never come. Down and down, back to the shadows and to the shuffling sounds of the bison and the bears, and the wolves I knew so well.

Back home.

Toomey would be there, of course. Waiting.

But you knew that. It's how the story ends, after all.

I told you at the start, so you knew what to expect, because I said John was dead and I killed him, and that was the truth. No fancy storytelling will ever change that.

And there were a lot of stories back then, and most of them were wrong, but that didn't stop them.

Local Man Killed in Stand-off

Woods Gunman Was Ex-Army

Dead Man Leaves Wife and Child

Gunman's Son Tipped-off Police, Claims Source Close to Family

Woods Siege Ends in Shoot-out, at Least One Dead

It was the dog, Mol. If it hadn't been for her, I'd have stayed in town, got to the payphone, made my call to the cops. I might have met up with John where we'd planned. Might have made it to Scotland, to that croft where me and Mam and John would have lived and bred goats and chickens and cooked fish, and Sophie would have come later, too. And all would have been fine.

But the dog had turned up, and I loved her and couldn't leave her now.

She'd come that day in the woods, come out of the shadows, like she'd always been there. Come up out from the earth, to be with me, to shape things. But she came from the wild and I couldn't hide her in town and I couldn't disappear when I had her. She wasn't a bear or a bison or a wolf, just a dog. Because it was men like Toomey and John that were the real wolves.

People like me.

THIRTY-ONE

I DIDN'T SEE THE Range Rover. He'd been sly enough to leave it up at Derby's place, slipped snug in a barn, gleaming unseen while he'd hiked down into the woods alone. He'd come prepared this time, in top-brand walking boots that would have cost as much as the bike John had bought from Benny. A black suit with a sheen, and white shirt. He would have watched me as I went down the stream, with Mol stumbling after me. He'd have watched how careful I was being, wary of making a noise. He would have seen me stop every twenty yards to check my watch. He would have seen the worry on my face as it got closer to the time, and me nowhere near the payphones we'd planned.

I hadn't had a choice, of course.

Say what you like, what with the SUV in town, the payphones were out of bounds, so there was only one way to make the call.

But first I texted John.

I typed in the number John had scribbled on a bit of paper for me last night, and texted . . .

Toomeys men in town. Pick me up near woods. Quarry.

Don't ask me why I waited to press send. Maybe I sensed the disaster that was coming, and this was the point to turn back. The point where the outcome might have changed. They say there is one in every tragedy – some place where you could have made a different decision, this one clear turning point. Only, in real life, it's not like that, is it? There are countless points, not just one, choices that get made without anyone really thinking, and you can't control it and you can't stop it. It's just what it is. And right then there was no way around it, I told myself. Because what else could I do?

Once I'd sent the text I called the police, and I waited to be put through. Not long, I told myself. Not long. Nearly done. Nearly over. The mantra in my head like a song I'd never finish.

'Hello? Yeah, there's a man on a bike. He's driving real fast. He'll kill someone—'

The woman on the line, the operator, she tried to stop me and ask my name. She was very polite about it. But John had told me they'd do that, trying to stall me, get information. So I just kept on saying the same thing over and over again.

'Listen to me, there's a man on a bike. He's driving real fast. He'll kill someone. Heading to Leeds. Leeds Road. You need to look for him.'

I was saying it for the third time, and just about to hang up, when Mol barked.

She must have seen him, you see. Or smelled him. She knew what I didn't. She recognised the danger hiding there amongst the trees, and so she barked, loud. For me and for John. Loud enough for the operator to hear. Loud enough to be recorded and played later at the inquest when it was all over and done and John was dead.

The sound of a dog and a boy, in the woods.

I shut off the phone, but not quickly enough. The damage was done.

'Shut up, girl,' I hissed.

But Mol wouldn't shut up. She stared blindly into the trees, standing stock-still, and she barked over and over. Making a racket. Raising hell.

I stared after her, not knowing what was wrong. I looked to the lines of shadow in the woods, to the dark.

'Who is it?' I called, trying to sound brave.

There was just the trees and the light between, and the sparkle of pollen and dust spreading against the blackness.

'Show yourself.'

A shimmer in that shadow, no more than a murmur. Not enough to be a man, I thought. And for a moment I was stupid enough to imagine Sophie had come. Lovely Sophie.

I grabbed Mol's neck, trying to hold her back. 'Stop, girl,' I told her. 'Stop it.'

'Told you she liked me.'

I saw the boots first, the shiny nap of the trousers tucked into the high leather collars.

'You can let her go,' Toomey said. 'Your old bitch won't hurt me, you'll see. I have a way with them.'

He stepped out of the young ferns, his narrow, tanned face beaming at me, laughter lines at his eyes, thick as spider's webs. 'You all right, lad? You look pale, like you've seen a ghost.'

Mol kept pulling and so I let her away, and she crossed the shallow ditch, and moved slowly, carefully into the ferns, nosing after Toomey's new boots. She was dead quiet, and placid, the alarm in her all gone for now, just like he'd anticipated.

'See?' he said, smiling. There was a white square of cotton taped above his left eye, a mean black craze of stitching beneath, the bloom of a bruise against the side of his face where John had clouted him. He looked down at Mol, let her smell his hand. 'Do you want to know the secret? If you want a dog to like you, you let it get close and you win its trust. You let it know it's safe. Once it thinks it's safe, you can do what you like with it. Hit it, kick it, whatever. Really go to town.' He scratched her behind her ear, and his smile widened.

I felt sick looking at him. I wanted to drag Mol away, but she was too old and too tired to run. I'd get away all right. I was quicker than a man like Toomey, and his boots would slow him down in the ditches. I knew the trees, and I knew the dips in the ground, the way it rolled and rose and how the heave of earth beneath gave way as though to trap you and pin you down. There was clay here, and sand, and every sort of soil, and I knew it all like the back of my hand. But Mol couldn't follow, and Toomey realised as much.

He caught her by the scruff and roughly patted her nose.

'Where's your old man?' he asked, still looking down into Mol's trusting face. 'No good trying to protect him, you know. He did something wrong and he'll have to pay. That's the way of the world. He knows it, and so do you.'

Did something wrong? Wait until you find out he's robbed you, you bastard, I wanted to tell him.

He was talking real calm, but he'd stop after every other word and roll his tongue against his gums, and I guessed John had knocked out one of his teeth, and I felt glad.

'You and me,' he said, glancing up so that a shard of sun dashed his face, dappled and watery. 'We don't have any grudge, do we? Everything's sweet between us, right? But me and your old man's a different matter. Things will be settled once he's faced up to it, but he'll have to pay, it's only fair.'

His eyes tilted down to my belt, to the knife. I'd brought it with me, for luck, for courage. The knife John had cast for me. My hand had gone to it, without me thinking. Its cold handle, the leather, pressed tight in my fingers.

'Doesn't have to be hard,' he said, smiling. 'We're not like John, are we? We can talk things out, nice and peaceful.'

'I'm not telling you where he is.'

'I didn't think you would. Not straight away. You wouldn't be much of a son if you did.' He reached into the pocket of his jacket, and dragged out a long black lead and looped the end over Mol's head. 'Do you know what collateral is?' he asked. 'It's like holding onto something until a fella finishes a job, something of value. You fellas don't have much, but what you do have means something to you, doesn't it? Like this old girl here.'

'Don't you dare do anything to her,' I said, the words catching in my throat, making me gag. I was frozen, feet planted hard on the ground like they'd taken root and might never move again. My eyes stung with hate. 'Just let her be.'

'I've got no use for a half blind old bitch,' Toomey said, laughing. 'She wouldn't even make good glue. So, once you tell me where to find John, you can have her and no bother.'

'I can't. I don't know where he is.'

The lazy light on Toomey's face shifted as a breeze blew in the branches above.

'It's true,' I said. 'I don't know.'

'It's not that I like to hurt animals,' he said. 'Some blokes do, but I'm not one of them.'

'Please, just let her go.'

'Some blokes get a thrill from it. Small men, mostly, so they need something smaller than them to suffer. Even if it's just some poor old mongrel.'

'Please,' I said, begging.

'But me, I just do it for business. I get no pleasure from killing anything. Live and let live, I say.'

His words were all bullets in the dark, all aimed at me. And Mol standing there, all still and trusting, with the lead around her neck.

'I'll tell you,' I said, finally. 'I'll tell you, just let her go.'

'Good lad,' he said, then.

THIRTY-TWO

I KNOW HOW STORIES work.

I tell you where we lived and what we did and how we survived. And our names. Things that people like to know when they read a story. And you'll be happy all right, and you'll build your picture and you'll judge what was right and what was wrong, and what doesn't fit. But there'll be other things that will stay unsaid, because some things I don't even know myself, like the whys and hows.

Why Toomey? Why did he come into our life? Why did I have to keep Mol and love her? Why couldn't John come back from the war and live with Mam and be happy with life like before?

Why did he have to die?

Knowing doesn't change a thing, see. Knowing won't bring him back. So what's the point of stories, but to tell the truth and try to show up the lies?

This is the truth: I told Toomey John was on his way and where to find him, so I betrayed him. And I changed the pick-up point, so I got him killed as surely as if I'd shot him myself. But I didn't tell the police, and John never hit me, not once, no matter what the papers said after. He never hurt me.

It was Toomey. It was always him.

It was Toomey in the shadows. Toomey that woke those beasts. And Toomey who lunged forward from the dark that day in his posh boots and before I'd even put up my hands he'd hit me across my face, and then a second time. I'd already told him what he wanted to know, but that didn't stop him. Nothing would have stopped him that day, of course. It's all he knew – violence and revenge and blood.

Mol barked and snapped. He was still holding her by the lead, and she pulled it from his hand and went for him. I'd never seen her like that before, never seen such teeth and snarling. Suddenly, there was blood on Toomey's white shirt, and the knife was in my hand.

The blade painted red.

Then he was leaning back, the knee of his trousers torn and stuck between Mol's jaws. His eyes wide and white, not knowing which was the bigger threat – me or the dog.

I can't tell you when Toomey broke away from her, but by then I'd managed to get to my feet, too. I couldn't see straight. There was a rage of pain in my head, and a mess of darkness, white and black flashing, shadow and sunlight. Toomey was swept to his knees, and then his boots went out, flailing at Mol's face. Another moment and I saw a rock in his hand, and heard a yelp. Then they were running through the woods, Toomey screaming anger and Mol a streak of yellow.

I was alone. I heard birds all about, and the rush of branches. Sharp stabs of pain split my face, made me see stars. I slipped the knife back in my belt and staggered across the uneven ground, and stopped again, trying to breathe.

'Mol!' I said, as loud as I could manage, which wasn't loud at all because all my words seemed to be stuck inside me and wouldn't come out.

I thought I heard a voice behind, not words exactly, a groan, a gurgle. It might have been John waking and going outside to howl at the sky. It might have been a stag or a bear. I couldn't see anything beyond the stripes of sun. But the voice – it continued low, like it was coming out of the earth. It was as heavy as a weight tilting down, a wrecking ball of hate, and now there came the smell of iron, of blood. I shook my head, tried to see clearer. And then there was Mol's bark out towards the quarry.

I set off through the trees, and it was like all the evil of the place was there, clogging the air as I ran, down into the gully with the flattened weeds where the white-tailed deer would lay, and then back up the slope, climbing until I felt the blood hiss in my ears, and suddenly the barbed wire fence of the quarry rose up, and there was Toomey against the crumble of rock and sandstone. And Mol facing him.

And behind them, rearing up – not shadow exactly, not dark—

Something alive and roaring, crackling the air as it came. An animal of fog and dirt that lumbered above Toomey's unseeing face. An ancient thing, older than the woods, and taller than timber or tree. I couldn't see its face at first, just the great hide of it, humped and bristled with hair. The sun picked out its horns, then blinded me to what happened next.

But I heard it.

I heard Toomey's scream, and when I'd blinked the light from my eyes, he was flat to the ground, an arm twisted and crooked behind his back and his head fixed at an ugly angle. An immense thing was pressing down, crushing him. I knew he was dead as soon as I heard the spent whistle of his lungs.

Nothing alive could make such a noise.

It took some minutes before I could find my bearings. Maybe I'd passed out, because Mol was beside me now, licking my face. Beyond the fence, Toomey's body lay like before, flat to the ground, crumpled and unmoving. I climbed up and walked across towards him, and stopped. I didn't want to go nearer. I could see enough. The heap of clothes, the matter inside all cracked and beaten down, and the crown of his head untouched, loose curls of hair and tanned scalp glinting with sun. One hand was flung out, the fingers bent as though they still held the rock that had struck Mol.

'Girl,' I said, checking her head for a gash or a wound, some cake of blood there. But she was unharmed.

189

And her eyes, those silvered discs, stared open and honest and gentle at me, as though Toomey had never happened.

In the distance a bulldozer went its weary way, the bulk of the steel bin raised and trailing so much dirt that it poured down like water.

I pulled the mobile from my pocket, looked at the time. It was ten minutes before me and John were supposed to meet up. There were no texts from him, but Sophie's name was there.

You OK? Tell me if you're safe.

A second text:

Is everything OK? Text if you can.

My brain wouldn't work properly. My thoughts tumbled and spun, unable to fix on a single place to land. What was it I'd seen? Was it the bison John had told me about? Had I just witnessed the great beast kill Toomey? I knew it was impossible, but then nothing seemed real, except the pain in my skull where Toomey had hit me. I reached up and looked to my fingers. There was blood on them.

Mol's wet muzzle against my cheek.

'Good girl,' I muttered. 'Beautiful girl.' I reached my arm around her neck and buried my face in her and sobbed. If I'd known it would be the last time I'd hold her, maybe I'd have clung on longer, maybe I'd never have let her go and wander back into the ferns and undergrowth.

I was still crying when I heard the motorbike approach.

THIRTY-THREE

On the far side of the trees, against the ragged line of the quarry edge, was the bike, its back tyre throwing up so much orange dirt it looked like it was on fire.

John.

He'd done it. He was here.

You have to remember I wasn't thinking clearly. My head was still rattling from Toomey's clout. I pulled myself along the line of wire, picking up my pace as the bike roared past.

I yelled. 'John!'

It was on a ridge parallel to me, spraying earth, John's face hidden by the black visor of the helmet. I waved and he pulled alongside, his back wheel skidding in the dust. He was no more than ten feet away, close enough for the exhaust fumes to catch in my throat. I smelled burned oil and rubber, and the heat of the bike flushed my face. John came to a halt, the engine still rumbling. He flipped up the visor. His eyes were pink, lines of sweat running down the length of his nose, making him look old and tired.

'Get out of here!' he screamed.

I was getting ready to climb up onto the seat behind him, eager to go. But he threw out his hand to stop me and pointed into the distance.

'Just go: Forget the plan, it's over.'

'What's happened? John?'

The bike turned, spun, kicking up rocks. John yelled at me. 'Get to your mam's.'

'No, I'm coming with you,' I said, jumping down into the ditch that separated us.

'You have to go. It's gone bad, all of it. The coppers'll be here. They called them. I'm sorry, I have to leave.' He revved the engine, and the bike spat out dirt, and lunged forward then stopped again. 'I'm sorry,' he repeated.

I watched as he sped off back the way he'd come. I ran after him for a few yards, then looked around, as though there might be an answer written in the dirt and clay left behind. But there was just a dim smudge of oil where the bike had been, and the slow-settling dust.

He hadn't even seen Toomey's body, I thought. He hadn't asked whether I was OK, hadn't said anything about the blood on my face.

I didn't know what to do, but my body was shaking, full of a buzzing need to move.

Like I was a ticking bomb that might go off any moment.

I followed the bike, and fell into a jog, and soon I was running as fast as I could, leaping over the rocks and weeds, skidding on the track and back into the shelter of the woods. The bike's engine echoed through the trees. It flashed and sparked on the horizon, black against the sun. The only other colour was a small pinprick of blue that suddenly appeared in the corner of my eye. It glimmered at the far end of the woods, no bigger than a gunflash.

The blue scattered against the black trunks in front of me. The broken glass of blue splitting, spinning.

The brightest blue you could ever see.

Police beacon blue.

Then I heard the sirens.

THIRTY-FOUR

THERE WERE TWO police cars. Big ones, the size of Toomey's Range Rover, painted white with yellow and blue checking on the sides.

They were accelerating down the access lane from the quarry to Derby's farm, trailing John's bike, which was smoking now. Thick black plumes billowing from the exhaust. I saw the bike falter and there was a loud *CRACK* that sounded through the trees, and another sputter of smoke, then John pulled a turn back into the shelter of the woods, so sharp it looked like he might come off.

The back wheel jacked up in the air, and I saw John's body thrown high. I heard the thud of him strike the ground. The police cars swept past, trailing a cloud of dust that coloured the sky brown. More police cars were coming now, and the sound of sirens split the sky.

I was struggling my way through the thick undergrowth, high as my waist. I couldn't get any closer.

The cars had parked up now and police officers were moving down through the trees, calling out to John to give himself up. Four of them. But John was nowhere to be seen. Nearby, the bike was still turning over and over, across the rough ground, wheel over wheel, as if in slow motion, before crashing down, finally, in a wheeze of choking petrol.

A clatter of ferns, and here was John.

He was red-faced and grey at the same time. Too much and too little colour for one face.

Lips blue, he said, 'Jesus, son.'

And I was frozen by so many things, I couldn't tell which had me most afraid. His look, the fearful sound of him, or the fact that he had called me 'son'. Because he never did, and he never had. This was the first time, and to me it signalled love, and it signalled danger.

In my mind it signalled the end of things.

Son. The beginning and the end, all at once.

And us two, in the woods, just two blokes. And it could have been any time and any forest and any two men who had ever lived.

'You have to go,' he said, his eyes wild. He'd lost his helmet, and clutched hard in his left hand was the strap of the rucksack. I saw money inside, crumpled paper in different shades of blue and brown.

In his right hand was the shotgun.

'Give me it,' I told him. And he looked at me, confused, not knowing which I meant. 'The gun. Please, John. Give it.'

He pulled it back close to him, pressed it to his ribs, greedy for it.

'Get out of here before they see you,' he said. He meant the coppers, the police, the enemy. But his face said, *It's mine and you'll never have it*.

The gun. The money.

Mine.

He didn't see the knife in my belt, or its tip beaded in Toomey's blood. He no longer saw the love in my face, or the fear. But he saw a son, at least.

This is what I told myself when I looked across to the coppers in the distance. I watched their silhouettes scatter amongst the trees, set wide against us, not coming but holding off, like an army awaiting orders. I was his son.

'John, no,' I said, one last time. I intended it to be one last time, although in the next thirty minutes I would say it many more times, to him, to myself, to no one. The same empty words – *John, no*.

'Remember what I told you about weak men?' he said, his voice quiet and broken. He was dry-mouthed, and the grey sweat on his skin shone livid, like old scars. 'Well, being a fighter doesn't make you strong, you get that, right? It didn't with me, it made me weak, is the truth. And that grandad of mine, he was the weakest man I knew, because he didn't care about anything. Pride was all he had, and he beat it out of whoever he met. But a strong man doesn't have to do that. You know that, don't you?'

I nodded. 'John—'

'On the coast, in the water, in the dark – you were fine,' he said, interrupting me. He was talking low, but his eyes were bright and searching, hectic with emotion. 'You didn't need me to pull you out. You'd have done it on your own. You can do anything, son.'

I tried to say something, but he stopped me. 'So you let me go now, because I'm on a different path. It's not your path, or Mam's, but mine.'

'I don't want to,' I said.

'I'm not giving you a choice.'

'No!' I yelled. And the coppers must have heard, because they started in our direction now, calling out John's name, telling him to stay calm.

'Give yourself up, *please*—' I told him.

But he wasn't listening. His ears were filled with the rage of blood again, and without another word, he scrambled down into the undergrowth, dragging the rucksack behind him, and taking cover behind a tree.

It was an ash, the tree, and without me beckoning them, John's lessons come back all at once: good fuel timber, ash. In the past, folk would look to the ash to heal their sick children. They would strip it and pass them through a gap in the trunk, and hope that they would be cured and blessed and happy.

I tried to follow him, but each time I got closer, he moved away, further into the thicket. 'Go!' he yelled. The blue lights kept turning and flashing, and the holding line of coppers did not shift. It was quiet enough now to hear the birdsong. As quiet as the wood ever was. So quiet you could let yourself believe nothing would ever happen if we stayed like this, and no man would ever move.

I remembered what John had said about war and prison.

Waiting. The trick was always in the waiting.

And that's when the fear returned. Because I knew how good John was at waiting, and I knew that no matter how long the coppers stayed standing there, he would stand longer. All his life, that's what he'd done. Iron John. Too stupid and stubborn to fall down.

He would remain standing even if it hurt, even if it wounded. Even if it killed.

He would not go down. I knew that.

Not until he was taken down.

Because eventually, even the greatest creature finds a better, I told myself, watching as a new vehicle arrived at the edge of the woods. More men were appearing, patient men, with guns of their own. They were taking up positions.

I remembered that stag trapped in the trees by its own twelve-point antlers, and I pushed myself through the ferns again, wrestled past the bracken and branches.

John saw me, and started.

He raised his hand to me, the

one holding the gun. I saw the two deep black eyes of the barrels. John aimed the shotgun at me, daring me to come closer. Wild John.

But, of course he wasn't. Aiming at me, I mean. It was Mol he was looking at, only I didn't know it, not then. She appeared out of the undergrowth, see, yellow as sunlight, taking his eye. It was her making him start. Making him jerk.

And a gun went off.

And me, now, I didn't think, *Bastard*.

No anger, not even fear.

Just numb.

I wanted to be back in the van, back asleep, back with John. I wanted to hear him wake and dress and walk out into the light and moan like a deer. I wanted all these things in the moment it took for the rifle to be trained on him and for a silent flash to spark beyond the ferns.

THIRTY-FIVE

WHEN YOU SEE someone die, afterwards it's hard to put it all back in the right order. The memories, I mean. Mam says memories are like a broken mirror, and you don't always have to put the pieces together perfectly to see properly. Which is true, but some things stick out and make me doubt myself. Like, I have this memory of John squatted down in the ferns, half hidden, and I can see the barrels of the shotgun pointing to the sky, and John holding it with his head bent down, like he was praying or something. And maybe I've made a noise, cracked a branch under my boots. And he looks up, to me. And he nods.

And that's when the shots ring out. The coppers. When they shoot him. When he dies.

I can see it now, clear as day, can see his cragged face. And he's not angry, or hate-filled. There's no bitterness or confusion in his eyes, just that calm from before.

But, you see, it's not true. It's a dream, that's all.

This is what they all tell me.

John aimed the gun at me, so the police had no choice. It's all on the video recordings the cops made. The ones they played at the inquest. And there's no mention of a dog. No dog was found injured. No sign she was even there. Just a new lead found left in the dirt by the quarry.

My counsellor says I dreamed it later – the thing with John praying – to make sense of it in my head, because I wanted to see him as a hero. That's what they say, that I hero-worshipped him. But I knew John wasn't a hero, and I always had. And he had no patience for heroes, did John.

The thing about the dreaming is true, though. I never stopped dreaming about what happened that day. And in the dreams John's always calm, and not panicked, not surprised. Just calm, like he knew what was all coming to him, and he'd accepted it. I still dream – these vague, fractured dreams that make me kick in my sleep, like Mol used to. Like John. Running. Like I'm trying to escape. Detailed dreams that stay in my head like new memories. My counsellor says it's my mind trying to work out the puzzle, see, trying to fit together pieces that may never properly fit. That it's not my fault, he says, it's just how your head works.

John was running from the police after the robbery, and he holed up in the woods, and although he was warned by the coppers to put down his weapon, he continued to threaten me, and finally they fired. That's the story, what everyone agrees. The armed police had no choice but to shoot when they knew a civilian's life was in danger. A minor.

John was a danger, see, an armed criminal with a history of violence, a bloke who'd just held up a betting shop, so they had no choice but to eliminate the threat. It's all real clear when they say it.

But it's not how I remember it.

Because what the official report leaves out is how he looked after me. It leaves out the croft and Mam and John and me and the goats we'd have. It left out the fact that he fought for this country, that he was brave, that he was everything I would never be. It left out the way he'd yell in the mornings after he woke up, like a muntjac. It didn't mention the smell of the caravan, either, and the tick-tick of the rain dripping on the tin sheet. It didn't say how funny he was, how he could repair anything you gave him, how he knew every plant and mushroom and tree and bird.

It didn't say that I loved him, and he loved me.

And it left out the great beast that had arrived and crushed Toomey. Because they never could explain that. They never tried.

They never mentioned the bears and bison and wolves that woke up in the woods and broke us.

They just said it was my mind trying to make the trauma right. My mind that conjured up a beast as big as a bus with horns long and curved. But if they were all in my head, then how do you explain Mol? Because plenty of folk saw her, and no one denies it.

Toomey died all right, they tell me, but it was an accident. The quarry was fenced-off for a reason. It was dangerous, they say. So it was easy for a distracted driver on a bulldozer not to see someone who'd strayed into the hazard area. Toomey was just in the wrong place at the wrong time, they said. He'd come to the quarry after the robbery to confront John, and he was crushed by a digger and he died and that was that.

They've got all the answers, you see.

It's like I said – you can't tell grown-ups. They do what they like, no matter what, believe what's easiest to believe, and ignore the rest.

You can see how they think. If it's a toss-up between a man killed by an ancient bison or a bulldozer, what would you choose?

But the thing is, I saw it. So I know. And Mol does, too.

Not that I ever saw her again. Mam and Sophie tell me she probably ran off out of fear and got lost, and we'll put up posters, they tell me, we'll try to find her. But me, I think she went back to the ground where she'd come from, her job done. One of *them*. Because, you see, I saw the immense power staring out of the black, matted fur of those beasts, the blink of their eyes. I saw the centuries in those faces, and I knew straight away what they were. And I knew they hadn't come to destroy me but to save me. And now I know, too, that it was John that had conjured them up, and that's why he had to die. Because like Toomey said, you have to pay for the things you do. You get nothing for nothing.

John knew that, and now so do I.

THIRTY-SIX

'WHERE DO YOU want to go?'

This is Thursday, after my appointment. Mam's here and we're walking home, and she tells me we can go anywhere I want at the weekend, her treat. Because of how well I'm doing. She means the counsellor, because he says there's nothing to stop me going back to school next week, if I feel up to it. His name's John, too, but he's nothing like my John, and anyway he says he spells it without an h – Jon.

They couldn't be more different, the two of them. Not that I don't like him, it's just an unusual sort of relationship, talking to a stranger about stuff. Takes getting used to. But he says I'm doing Just Fine, and I should be Very Proud of Myself, which I don't get. Because what's to be proud of? But I let him go on with it all, and I say thank you, and to be honest it is good sometimes to just say what's on your mind and not have to worry about people hating or judging you. And he doesn't say it, counsellor Jon, but I get the feeling a lot of people think I should be back to normal now, and everything that happened, happened, and pull your socks up and get on with life. But it's not like that, and it never will be.

In town, I meet Sophie and we walk by the canal. There are cabbage whites and orange tips in the grass, and we stop to watch the petrol blue twist of kingfisher wing and tail skitter past so close to the water that it seems to slip briefly beneath the surface, in that other world beyond us, before returning as bright as paint.

'He loved you,' Sophie's saying. 'Whatever he did, he loved you.'

And I know it's true, course I do. But it doesn't mean I don't feel bad sometimes, and it doesn't mean I sleep any better.

Because I'm as rubbish at sleeping now as John was. So most days I get up early, and I walk out of the estate, and down to the canal and watch the day wake.

It's not like the woods, and there's too much concrete and iron and fencing for my liking. But it's enough for now. And birds don't see the rubbish and clutter, do they? To them the world is just the world, and we're just all passersby. Nature takes advantage of the neglect, and won't be stopped.

'Mam says I should plant a tree for him,' I say, once we've made it to the bushes by the lock, where the coots have nested. I can tell a coot from a marsh hen now. And I know a nuthatch from every sort of woodpecker, and I wonder how I could ever have confused them, because they couldn't be more different. 'She says he'd like that. You can come, if you want,' I say, looking to Sophie. 'It'll be an oak. It'll take twenty years before it grows its own acorns, but when it's full grown it could live for a thousand years.'

Sophie listens and doesn't say anything, which means she's thinking and so I wait.

'Do you ever wonder why it happened?' she asks, at last.

'Wondering won't change it,' I say. 'But yeah, sometimes I do. I wonder if he knew what would happen, if it was part of the plan.'

'Do you think he did?'

'I think in the desert he had mad happy dreams of what he'd do when he got back, and those dreams were as real to him as me or Mam, maybe more real. And he'd set his mind on making them true, no matter what it meant, or how it might end.'

'And what mad and happy dreams do you have?'

I shake my head and smile. 'I'm happy enough,' I say, and I feel Sophie's hand slip into mine and I want to tell her *this* makes me happy, her hand. This is happiness. And part of me wants to tell John, and show him Sophie, and tell him I'm all right.

And sometimes at night when I'm not sleeping, I do.

Because John's here and not here. He's dead but he's around at the same time, in the sad way Mam smiles at me, or when I feel the spit of rain on my back, or out in a field, with the larks warbling overhead. And he's never going to go now, not altogether, and Mam says that's good because nothing ever really does go away. It's all in us, all of the time, like he said.

But she's wrong.

Because Mol's never coming back, and the wolves have gone away.

At night I don't hear them turn underground any more, and the bear and bison have gone, too. And now it's so quiet I can't get to sleep because my head is full of my thoughts, and that's worse than them being there. And sometimes I dream there's just me and John and we're in the woods again, and he's stripping and washing the nettles for tea, while I light the fire to boil the water. And sometimes I think I hear him calling out like a muntjac, and it wakes me up, but I'm not scared, just sort of thoughtful and lost for a minute, because I'd forgotten he was dead.

'Can we go to the coast?' I say, making up my mind, later, when Sophie's gone and it's just me and Mam.

Mam says of course. And next day we catch the bus and watch in silence as hills heavy with heather pass by, and then through the front window on the top deck the first chalk line of sea appears, high above the town, impossibly high. And then the slow descent down the moorland road, and there are houses and trees and big old hotels with whitewashed walls, and then we've arrived with the sharp tang of salt and fish and a whip of wind in your face when you step out.

Later, we sit on the edge of the harbour, out on the spit of stone, so far out all you can hear is the sea and the call of birds out in the blackness above, and when I look up, just for a moment, beyond the cloud and beyond the deepening dark, I think I can see a star shine and right then it could be Gold and Stars I'm looking at, and I feel that something's gone, but some new thing is here, too, and it all swirls together, new and old, in that inky black.

And it will continue, now and for ever.

ACKNOWLEDGEMENTS

I'd like to thank Charlie Sheppard and Chloe Sackur for their invaluable help and support in guiding this book to publication. Many individuals influenced the art of *We Were Wolves*, but I'd like to name Charles Keeping, in particular, for the remarkable body of work that has inspired these and countless other illustrations.